The Island

A Novel by
Alasdair McPherson

A McStorytellers publication

http://www.mcstorytellers.com

Contents

Chapter One: *Pure Magic*

Speaking for myself, I don't think the truth would have come out if it had not been for Aunt Effie's little problem. She was really my great aunt and I did not even know she existed until I was nearly thirteen. That was when my Granddad died and I found out the secret truth about my family. My Gran had left a croft on the island to travel to Glasgow to train as a nurse; there she had met, been courted and, after observing all the mating rituals in force at the time, she married Granddad.

The trouble was that he, being a typical Glaswegian, small, thin and agitated by a perception that he was the smartest operator in the smartest city in the world, did not reckon any non-Glaswegians very highly. But he particularly despised the island Scots who, in his opinion, lived in hovels, spoke a strange language – heedrum hawdrums as he put it – and were as thick as mince. The tenement where my father and sisters were brought up was a long way short of Homes and Gardens and all his cleverness never earned him more than a pittance as a type-setter on the Herald, but his sense of superiority was innate.

He would not have described himself as a 'Glaswegian': "Am from Govan, get it?" Glasgow is considered by the natives to be a loose confederation of villages with their own history and customs: not 'customs' as in border controls, you understand, although the idea is not without merit: try wearing a green and white scarf in Maryhill and you will see what I mean.

Govan is something of an anomaly. It is next to Gorbals,

geographically speaking but that village, despite the evidence of teeming humanity, is uninhabited: everyone lives in Govan, home to Glasgow Rangers and perfectly respectable. You only say you come from the Gorbals if you want to cultivate a reputation as a hard man; the other way is to claim to be a graduate of the Bar-L. You give your home village as Govan to show you have a bit of class.

My Gran was, I later discovered, a typical islander: she marched to her own band. She never questioned Granddad's estimate of her intelligence but, by the time I was born, she was earning more than him as a theatre sister. She never spoke Gaelic about the house although she told me later that not only did she say her prayers in the old tongue, she taught her children to do the same!

She had left behind a brother, James, who still lived on the croft as he had done all his life except for a spell during 'the War' when he reached the rank of Lieutenant Commander in the Royal Navy with command of a destroyer or a cruiser or something even bigger and more important. I sort of assumed she meant World War II partly because Gran seemed ancient but partly because that was the only war I had ever heard of!

She had never openly defied Granddad's aversion to his brother-in-law, but she kept up an intermittent correspondence with his wife, Effie. Gran wrote to this woman who had married her brother although they had never met.

"If I'm right," she told me, "I think I remember her as a plump wee lassie with blonde plaits and a runny nose. Of course she's four years younger than me so I hardly noticed her at school."

Effie sent her letters to the Manse and the Minister's wife gave them to Gran when they shared flower duty in the church.

A month after Granddad died, Gran was having her tea with us when she announced that she was planning a visit to the island.

"They won't let you in," my Father said with his customary bluntness.

"They've invited me," Gran replied, quietly snaffling the last iced tea cake from right under Dad's questing fingers. He had a way of looking straight at you trying to mesmerise you into ignoring his hand questing for the plate of cakes. I had had an eye on it myself: it was really my Mum's but after humming and hahhing for ages she had finally renounced it as being bad for the figure.

After my Father got over the shock of finding that his Dad had been deceived for years, he was mockingly sceptical. He is a detective constable in the Glasgow Police and he shares his Father's disdain for the islander. Many of the uniformed officers were from the Highlands and they were widely believed to be as thick as mince.

Glasgow is the sink into which the Highlander pours when he leaves the croft. No sooner does he arrive than he gets nostalgic for hills and water. He quickly forgets that the hills are usually hidden by the rain and that much of the water finds its way down your neck when you venture out!

The thought of his own Mother travelling north to spend time with the natives shocked him and he was appalled to discover that she planned to travel alone. He used to tell me his Father's story that she had first arrived in Glasgow by mule train or in a covered wagon like in a Western, but he would not countenance a journey involving his Mother in boarding trains and ferries. After all, she had led a sheltered life. (He conveniently forgets that she worked in an operating theatre while he fainted the first time he witnessed an autopsy, or so she said.)

So it was that, three weeks later, he took four days leave to drive her to her childhood home. Since it was school holidays, I was included in the entourage. I was sick twice with pure excitement about going on such an epic journey but managed to hide it from Mum who had a tendency to wrap me in cotton wool at the best of times.

I had been out of the city before, of course: on one memorable day I paddled and squished my toes in the sand at Saltcoats. Once we passed Luss, however, I was in *terra incognito*. Granddad had a car and he used to take us for jaunts on a Sunday to Loch Lomond, provided Rangers had won on the Saturday. He was a little uncertain, however, about the exact location of reverse gear so as we approached Luss he would slow down and wheech round the tree at the top of the village street opposite the Colquhoun Arms and make the best of his way back to the dear green place. We would pull-in at the Duck Bay marina and feed the ducks while Granddad eased his hangover at the bar.

This time we went far beyond this boundary to find that, for me at least, there really was heaven in the Highland wiles and I did get to smell the tangle of the isles. Glasgow born as I was, I had never before questioned the miserable conditions that I had been told existed outside the city.

Uncle James met us at the croft gate, a tall ruddy complexioned man with a broad grin displaying a fine set of shop-bought teeth. He was dressed in a seaman's jumper with almost as many holes as wool over stained and torn jeans; his feet were encased in wellington boots with the tops turned down and on his head was a flat cap with a skip. Dad had on smart brogues with slacks and an Arnold Palmer golf jumper.

"Ah Jean, it's yourself," James greeted Gran as she stepped out of the car.

"That coo's lookin' a bit peaky," was her reply as she ran her hand over the flank of the patient bovine who formed the other half of the welcoming committee.

James' smile was replaced by a worried look and he turned away with, I thought, a tear in his eye: I must have been mistaken because grown-ups don't cry about cows, do they?

A small, wiry woman appeared at the croft door, drying her hands on her apron. This was Effie whose hair, now grey, was still in becoming plaits; she was no longer plump being inclined to wiriness and I was pleased to see that her nose had dried up. Any sorrow about the ailing cow was lost in the flood of welcomes and reminiscences. Apart from being exclaimed over, I was left out of things because Gran, James and Effie all spoke in Gaelic. To my utter astonishment, my Dad laughed at some of the jokes – when had he learned the despised language?

It was a magical few days even if the only Gaelic phrase I learned was *greas shuas*. In fact it went so well that Dad agreed to leave me there with Gran when he went back to work sorting out Glasgow hard men. He promised to come back to collect us in a few weeks and went off whistling a waulking song. He had no qualms about leaving his only son in this land of rain-sodden imbeciles, it seemed.

I ran wild for the next few days; there were so many things to do on the sea shore and up on the moors behind the croft. Did it rain? It may have, but it certainly did nothing to spoil my time on the island. When I got back to the croft, Gran or Aunt Effie would get up, feed me and then settle back into their armchairs across the grate, knitting and gossiping in the aromatic haze of the peat fire, as if they had been friends for a lifetime. After I ate I could go back out and talk to Uncle James until night fell. It was never totally dark in these summer nights but the stars were visible and he would show me the constellations and spin stories of navigators who circled the globe with little more than the stars and an accurate chronometer.

"Of course, Eric the Red," he went on, knocking his pipe out against the heel of his wellington. "He discovered America with nothing more than a compass shaped like a little fish – a lodestone they called it."

"I thought Christopher Columbus discovered America."

"A Johnnie-come-lately, yon fellow Columbus. Eric found the place and called it Vinland. They colonised it too but sickness drove them out."

He paused to light his pipe before he went on. "Then there was an Irish monk, Brendan I think they called him, who set out to find Tir nan Og, the island of youth, but ran into America instead. Funny now that all these Hollywood stars are still looking for eternal youth."

I was accustomed to glottaly stopped Glasgow Scots but Uncle James and his friends spoke clearly and quietly with nothing more than a pleasant burr. They always had time to spare and never treated me like the annoying kid I probably was.

Bedtime was when I gave in to tiredness and went upstairs to my little box room that housed a squeaky single bed and a battered dining chair. Next morning, I rose when I pleased: no adult told me to rest or rise, wash or eat, although I was expected to bring water from the well without being told and to make sure the scuttle was filled with peats. We had water piped in, of course, but Aunt Effie would only drink tea made from water from the old well.

It was some days before I heard any more about the sick cow. She was the only one left and they kept her as much out of sentiment as for her milk, although she did provide for their small needs. Sadly, her udders had shrunk and her teats were not much bigger than walnuts.

It was a wet night so the fire was burning brightly and we were all sitting in the main room. Uncle James and I were at the dining table where he was showing me how to tie a hook to a fishing line while the ladies were in their accustomed places, knitting and chatting in the flickering firelight.

They were talking about the cow and I could tell that Uncle James was listening although he said nothing still deftly attaching hooks. Then Aunt Effie looked across at him and raised her voice.

"We've seen the vet but he just shakes his head and asks what can we expect at her age? I've asked him," she nodded her head in the direction of James. "I must have asked him a hundred times to get his friends the wizards to do something. But will he? Not him!"

Uncle James placed the hooks carefully on the table and then rose without a word going out through the rain to the byre with me on his heels.

"Did Aunt Effie say wizards?" I shrilled, with my eyes, no doubt, as big as saucers. At first he would say nothing but after a time he sat me on a hay bale, one of a few he had bartered for a lamb, and told me the whole story.

In the old times, the township had taken the sheep across to an uninhabited island at the mouth of the harbour to graze for the summer. When he got back from the Navy, the government had taken possession of the island and had built a mysterious research station on it. The old men were incensed and wanted to go to law to get their grazing back but James had spent five years getting to know the official mind and he proposed another solution. He approached the Director of the colony, put it to him that the villagers had suffered a material loss and asked for the contract to supply the island in perpetuity.

After a bit of negotiation, a deal was struck that satisfied everyone. The villagers got new boats and a steady income so they were able to give up the chancy business of keeping black-face sheep although most of them, including James, kept twenty or so ewes just, as he put it, to keep their hands in.

It was not long before the purpose of the research was known to the villagers. Some bright spark in Whitehall had read about witchcraft in the Middle Ages. Then he came across an article saying that in Africa people cursed by the witch doctor would sicken and die. He convinced the government to fund a research centre where people would learn spells and practice magic. He believed that if they were kept well away from sceptics and worked in an atmosphere of total belief they would develop magical powers. The resulting army of warlocks and witches would undoubtedly win any future war.

He argued that if people really believed in magic then it would happen. So, about thirty years before, the island was fitted out with every modern convenience with the exception of newspapers, radio and television. Since the villagers did not want to lose an easy and lucrative living supplying the wizards and witches, they kept their knowledge of what was going on in the outside world to themselves. After all it was no more far-fetched than kelpies and they all knew of babies who had been abducted by them!

Uncle James was now put in a quandary by Effie's remark. He loved the old cow and he loved his wife even more. On the other hand he was reluctant to break the unspoken agreement not to notice what went on at the research centre. I think he only told me because he needed an audience while he reasoned out his next move.

For the first and only time on the island, he sent me to bed. Next morning when I got up he had already sailed for the colony taking only the old cap that Effie wore when she rested her head against the cow's flank as she was milking. He knew some of the methods of the wizards: they needed something belonging to the beast before the magic would work and the old cap was matted with hairs from the cow.

It was a day or two before anything noticeable happened. Then the cow started eating better and looked a lot livelier. Within a week her udders had filled out, her teats hung proudly down and the milk yield was higher than it had been in her youth.

I was the first to notice the other change having just reached the age when I had become aware of the opposite sex. Effie was still thin but she had become sprightlier, bursting into fits of giggles for no apparent reason. It was not this that attracted my attention: her bust had become more prominent and a great deal shapelier. She confided in tears to Gran that she had begun leaking milk.

We had all forgotten that the milking cap also carried some of Effie's hair!

Chapter Two: *Festina Lente*

Six weeks after my Gran was reconciled with her brother James, she put her house on the market and moved to the island where she bought a property in the capital. As with many capitals around the world, it is hard to say where the centre ends and the suburbs begin. On the island what you might call the greater capital area including the suburbs is about as big as a small village. There are marginally fewer sheep cropping the roadside grass in the commercial centre than in the suburbs.

House prices there are modest so Gran was able to exchange her Partick flat for a much roomier place with a shop underneath. She swapped her view of other red-sandstone tenements and streets slick with rain and chip wrappings for a picture window overlooking the harbour with the hills in the distance. She could even discard her alarm clock since she could not sleep through the gulls following the lobster boats into the haven at five in the morning – except on the Sabbath, of course; seagulls are noisy at any time but with food in prospect they could wake the dead. They had to be back early so the skipper would be on time for his day job while the crew got ready for school.

Before Easter the shop had been re-wired, decorated and fitted with rudimentary tables covered in sparkling checked clothes starched to the point where you had to score them with a blunt knife to bend them to fit. The chairs were expensive wheel-backs in a matt, dark varnish. The floor was carpeted in bold black and white checks.

"Guaranteed not to show any marks," Gran told me when she

showed me round. "You just give it a wipe with a soapy cloth and it's as good as new. The man demonstrated with everything I could think of from cooking oil to blood.

"When I think of all the years I spent scrubbin' linoleum floors. Talk about keepin' women chained to the house!"

It came as a surprise to me that she had ever had lino' on the floor: all the time I knew her she had fitted carpets! I slipped away before Gran started blaming me for the centuries of pain that men have inflicted on the weaker sex: "Weaker sex, is it – no man that ever lived could endure what us women do!"

I suppose she must have been talking about the old days, because in my experience men do what women tell them – or else! In those days I thought my Mum and Dad were really old so Gran and James were like people from history.

Gran and Aunt Effie opened their tearoom on Good Friday, promising special cream teas and all-day breakfasts.

"Bloody Hell, Gran," I said when she told me the plan.

"I'll wash your mouth out with soap if I hear any more of that filthy language!"

I was thirteen years old (nearly fourteen if you want to be picky!), for goodness sake, and at a secondary school where saying 'hell' would have marked you out as a namby-pamby mother's boy. I was no tough but you had to stand up for yourself or be mowed down, as my Dad was always telling me. We lived in Whiteinch, a 'good' area, meaning that knives were rarely used in ordinary playground disagreements! An ability to swear fluently was almost as important as a willingness to exchange blows in winning you playground cred.

But when your Dad was in the polis you had to be prepared to stand your ground. An ability to swear fluently was almost as important as a willingness to exchange blows in establishing your credibility.

"You got the place cleaned up really quick, Gran," I said thinking a bit of verbal soft soap might help her to forget the threatened use of the more robust sort. "I thought the islanders were supposed to be a bit dilatory."

"Did you leave your brains back in your school bag? It is pace that matters, not speed – and you can stop glowerin' at me as if I was talking Gaelic.

"It is true that the islanders will find time to chat to their friends when there is no urgency – my Father used to say that when God made time he made sure there was plenty of it. You foreigners from Glasgow are always saying the pace of life is slow on the island. But come a storm at sea and the islanders will have the lifeboat out before you can blink. Whatever the weather, they never stop to ask if the folk in trouble even deserve to be rescued.

"Then again, who do you know back in the city that will get up at two in the morning to gather whelks before the tide comes in? See that lobster boat at the pier? Her skipper landed a catch by half past five and then went off to drive the school bus. While the bairns are learning he'll mend the creels and be back at the school gate with a smile on his face when they get out."

Hang on a wee minute, I thought. You have spent most of your life in Glasgow so when did you become public relations director for the island life?

She had been walking around the tearoom all the time fiddling with the tablecloths or moving a chair a millimetre or two. Finally she looked around with a quiet nod of satisfaction and went through the beaded curtain into the staff area to put on the kettle for a wee *strupuach*.

"Pace, you see: go slowly, take it easy when you can, but be ready when there is a need to pour on the speed. My shop needed doing so I just talked Alasdair Electrics into giving it priority. Mind it helps that I know a few words in Gaelic that he had never heard before: not from a sweet old lady, at any rate!"

"They knew all about pace even in ancient Rome. *Festina lente* they said – hasten slowly."

Turning to James, who had just walked through the back door, she asked, "Would that be Virgil do you think?"

"Not at all, not at all: that was Suetonius talking about the Emperor Augustus."

I was learning that speaking softly and rather slowly did not indicate rustic ignorance. Where else would you overhear two men, in rough clothing doing a menial manual task, discussing the implications of the Higgs boson – this at a time when the Hadron facility was only half built!

I had arrived with my Father late on Maundy Thursday to be shown the tearoom before it opened for business.

"Are they having an official opening ceremony," I asked my Dad when we had left the ladies to their last minute titivation of the premises.

"More like an official closing. It's Good Friday in the last stronghold of strict religious observance outside of Iran. They'll be lucky if they get the key turned before the local ayatollahs descend to call down divine retribution."

I was puzzled: Gran knew the island so she had to know the consequences of flouting the strict rules of behaviour.

"All publicity is good," Uncle James told me with a chuckle. "The girls reckon that the outrage of opening on Good Friday will make sure that everyone in a fifty mile radius will be talking about nothing else for the next week. The old biddies will tut and disapprove but they will make sure that they come in for a cup of tea. They'll be lookin' for things to criticise but I back Effie and Cissie to win them over.

"Even if they don't," he added after several minutes of silent contemplation, cleaning, filling and lighting his pipe. "It will give them good practice for when the tourists arrive – and that's where the money is."

We were getting the boat ready for a fishing trip out in the minch. The Laird had a business friend who was keen to do some deep sea fishing so James was going to take him to a spot under the cliffs where the currents slacken and deposit rich pickings for cod.

"Lazy cattle, cod, they want to swan about waiting for the food to come to them – not like the mackerel that swim faster than any other fish in the sea. Daft beasts, mind you: they are so greedy that they will swallow a coloured feather if it floats near them.

"Now cod will eat anything. You can always catch a nice rock cod near a sewer outflow."

This was not the happiest news for me because I had wolfed down three or four rock cod, fried in butter, when I arrived on the Thursday. The flesh is so firm and sweet that I could not believe that they had dined on sewage: I caught a twinkle in my uncle's eye.

James and I got on really well although he is nearly as old as Gran and she is sixty-seven. I could ask him anything and he would answer me gravely and thoroughly. Everyone in Glasgow either expected me to know things, or got impatient when I asked, or they told me I wasn't old enough to understand! Uncle James never made me feel stupid or naïve: an amazing skill in dealing with a thirteen year old who was both.

We were loading the boat with heavy duty hand-lines while we talked; the heads and guts of saith and rock cod were in a pail amidships for bait. I was amazed at the size of the hooks – they looked like grappling irons – five centimetres long and made of grey galvanised iron.

The Laird arrived just then with his guest.

"This is George McPhee, Philip. He is the Chief Executive of a knitwear company near Perth – they make an awful lot of jumpers for the Americans."

"Chief Executive," mused James shaking hands with a dumpy, rolly-poly man with iron grey hair and an even greyer expression. "Does that mean that you're the chief knitter then?"

The laird had a small coughing fit while we ran the dinghy down into the receding tide.

"Oh no! A Chief Executive doesn't actually make the goods," Mr McPhee confided with a laugh. "As a matter of fact all the knitting is done on machines – outsourced to India."

"But don't your advertisements say 'designed and produced in Scotland' and isn't there a picture of a wee old woman sitting knittin' in a shawl?" I wondered how Uncle James knew things like that about someone he could never have expected to meet?

Mr McPhee was amusingly dismissive of advertising material. He even confided that not only was the knitting done overseas, the designs were the work of a company in Birmingham.

We had a long way to row to reach the fishing grounds and there is only so much you can say about Scottish knitwear conceived, produced and sold outside our borders. It was, predictably, Uncle James who found a new topic.

"We used to have a wheen o' McPhees here spring and autumn when I was a lad. We're a wee thing later with our crops than the farmers down south so the Tinker McPhee clan would come to us when they were finished down there. They came to thin neeps in the spring and hauk tatties in the autumn. When they left us they went to their winter quarters – three nice Victorian mansions they owned near Dunoon.

"The women were hard workers and they kept the black tents warm and snug: dirty but comfortable. The men were a very different proposition; they used to do a lot of outsourcing, I can tell you!

"I mind one time I came out the bank – it must have been a Monday, washday, you know – and found one of the McPhees looking into a shop window. We exchanged a few pleasantries about the weather and the fishing and so on. Then I said: 'that's a nice shirt you have on – I have one just like it myself'. 'They mass produce them by the thousand,' says he without so much as a blush. 'I'm surprised that they mass produce so many with the same keel mark I got on mine when a braxy ewe couped me onto the pail of Stockholm tar I was using on the maggots'".

"What happened, Uncle James?"

"Nothing much: I went home with my shirt and he went home in his simmet."

Mr McPhee had gone a bit quiet while James was talking about his tinker namesakes. "I was maybe a thing harsh," my uncle told me later. "Some of our own ancestors were no better than they should be."

Luckily, we did well at the fishing: one of the two fish we kept weighed more than twenty pounds as Uncle James would have it (ten kilograms, as every good European knows).

It was a happier boat on the return home with Mr McPhee having recovered all his bounce.

"I have been admiring your sun tan," Uncle James remarked in a conciliatory tone.

"I'm just back from Spain. The wife and I spend as much time as we can at our villa – we were away for three weeks in March. It fair sets you up to get some warm sunshine away from the dark and gloom of bonnie Scotland. Of course we still have to heat our kidney-shaped swimming pool so early in the year but it is worth it."

He waxed lyrical about the climate and natural beauties of Spain but he was a lot less enthusiastic about the people. He had spent the whole three weeks waiting for someone to come to do a bit of electrical work on the villa, but to no avail.

"'Manana', they say. It means tomorrow in Spanish but their tomorrow never seems to come! Get on and do the job, is my motto in life! You Highlanders have a reputation for being dilatory. Is there a word in Gaelic that means the same as 'manana'?"

"So 'manana' means putting a job off for a day or so?" Uncle James lifted his cap and scratched his balding skull, frowning in concentration.

"No," he said eventually. "I don't believe there is a word in the Gaelic for such an emergency."

Chapter Three: *Special Cream Teas*

The tearoom proved to be an outstanding success. The opening on Good Friday passed off without incident because Gran and Aunt Effie offered free tea or coffee with a buttered scone to the folk who had been to church. Not only was it good business but sound theology – even if they did not provide any small fishes.

It would be an exaggeration to say that the locals flocked to the tearoom, but there were usually two or three tables occupied by matrons who had slipped in to nibble and delicately sip while they tried to maintain their disdain of store bought cakes. Of course, they knew that Gran did all the baking and they were prepared to admit, if pushed, that her scones were very nearly as good as their own baking!

Effie was in charge of the dairy products. Her cow, even revitalised, could not cope alone with the demand for cream and Effie's home-made yoghurt. Since everything they used was locally produced there were crofters all over the island rubbing their hands at the nest-eggs they were accumulating.

The tearoom was packed to the doors once the tourist season got properly under weigh. Uncle James and my Dad laid decking at the back door and we put out six tables so that customers could sit outdoors enjoying the views. A canopy kept off the rain although nothing could stop the wind that frequently blew in from the western isles. It had to pass over the pier and foreshore on its way but, speaking for myself, I like the tangy smell of dead fish and rotting seaweed.

Everything was going well: the ladies were rushed off their feet but they employed pupils from the high school as waitresses. The outfits of blindingly white, frilly blouses over black pencil skirts were very becoming. Of course the skirts were soon shortened and I know for a fact that Gran provided hold-up stockings with frilly tops that winked into view when the girls bent over to serve the customers at less than cost price.

It may have been this that accounted for more and more husbands developing a taste for tea and cake. I think the female customers benefitted: they got good tea properly brewed, delicious cakes, the company of their menfolk and young girls showing more than was proper for them to tut over

"Does your mother know you go out in public dressed like that?"

"Ay – and she told me about you and her in hot pants wi' these German hikers."

"Blethers! Come away, Donald, it's far too crowded in here."

The fly in the sugar bowl arrived in a business suit toting a black document wallet. He was one of those old young men; late twenties but with a settled complacent look, he was not fat but already beginning to lose his bloom, well on the way to swapping his six-pack for a firkin.

Gran came out of the back room when he enquired for the owner and she invited him to sit down at a table. He twisted his mouth into what he fondly imagined was a smile and gave his head a mock-regretful shake.

"I think you are the one who will need to sit down," he told Gran.

It turned out that he was from the Local Authority – the council. He did sit down, opened his smart imitation leather case and placed a substantial sheaf of papers on the table in front of him.

"You will have to shut," was his opening sally. He waved a hand to indicate the whole room and added: "Immediately."

"But it's only two in the afternoon," replied Gran.

"Ay, and we stay open 'til nine or ten this time of year," added Effie who had come out of the kitchen to see what was going on.

He gave a contemptuous little laugh. "No, no. I mean that you will have to close down altogether. You have no permission to open this café."

"Tearoom." Gran interrupted. "It's a tearoom, not a café."

"Café, tearoom, whatever you call it, you do not have permission for it – in fact I can find no record that you ever even applied for permission.

"You have changed the use of the building," he began to count the transgressions by tapping the fingers of his left hand with the index finger of his right. "You are preparing food in premises that have not been inspected, far less licensed, and you are getting supplies from sources that have not been approved by the council."

He sat back with an air of considerable self-satisfaction. You could nearly hear him thinking: "that will show the old biddies that they can't mess with the council or with me."

"He thought he had put our gas in a peep," as my Gran put it when she was telling James about it later.

At this moment Helen came to stand on the opposite side of the table with her wee pad in her hand and her pencil poised. She is a few years older than most of the girls, having just finished her second year at Glasgow University. She is tall with green eyes and beautiful auburn hair that she wears in plaits curled over her ears. (She told me it is because she loved Heidi when she was a kid, but she teases me all the time so she was probably joking.)

When she asked the man from the council what he wanted to order, he looked up ready, I am sure, to dismiss her summarily. Instead he encountered big green eyes over a smiling mouth – not to mention generous cleavage since the crafty minx had undone a couple of buttons on her blouse.

"Oh... ah... let me see? Just – perhaps – coffee...er... miss." Making a masterly effort he raised his eyes to hers and added: "That would be lovely."

He was blushing so fiercely that even his scalp was glowing through his thinning fair hair. The tearoom was fairly quiet in the lull between lunch and afternoon tea, but the eyes of the dozen or so customers were focussed on the embarrassed official. Hands were suspended between plate and mouth as they waited tensely for the next step to unfold.

He cleared his throat a few times while his colour returned to normal. "Would it not be better to continue this discussion somewhere more private?" he suggested.

"Not at all," replied Gran. She had remained standing so that, although she is not tall, she seemed to be looming over the seated man. "It is our customers that will suffer if you close us down so they have a right to hear what you have to say for yourself."

"Well, as I said, it's a matter of you opening this caf.., this tearoom, without permission." He made a visible effort to restore his self-confidence, patting the papers in front of him. "Public health is a very important matter, as I am sure you will agree. We – I – have a duty to protect the public from – well now, how can I phrase it? – unlicensed operators like yourself."

"I think he's sayin' that you might poison us, Cissie," one of the customers helpfully observed.

The discussion was suspended at this point by the entrance of Helen carrying a tray with coffee and a plate of the special cream scones. The fact that she had undone at least one more button on her blouse did not go unnoticed by anyone in the room. Not only was the lacy trim of her bra evident but there was a suggestion of more lace at her stocking tops since her skirt had been hitched up another two inches.

"Helen," Gran said, with a sweet smile. "Sit down here a minute will you lass? I know you are studying Public Health at the University so I think you could be a big help."

Helen pulled a chair round to sit alongside the council officer with her near-naked thigh pressing against his trouser leg.

"If I sit here it makes it easier for you to show me your papers and things. Now you drink your coffee before it gets cold and eat that lovely cream cake – it's our speciality, you know?"

She turned towards him and pushed his hair back over his forehead giving him a spectacular view of her bust.

"You look as if you need taking care of," she added, lifting the scone to his mouth and holding it while he ate, which he did with marked enthusiasm. When he was finished she caressingly wiped his mouth with her fingers.

This was too much: he jumped up, bright red and sweating, shoved his papers back into the document case and held it over his groin while he backed towards the door.

Regaining some composure he managed a parting shot. "Leave it with me. I am sure that something can be arranged." He made the mistake at this point of looking at Helen who gave him a seductive look and a little pout.

With that he turned and bolted out the tearoom, almost landing in a stroller being pushed along the street by a mother who pursued him until he was out of sight with a tirade of words she should not properly have used in front of a child.

Before the door closed behind him the customers exploded with laughter.

"Helen, you're a wee superstar," Gran said, hugging the grinning waitress.

I had watched the whole play from behind the beaded curtain enclosing the private kitchen area and I can tell you that I was as embarrassed and aroused as the official at Helen's antics – I could have done with a document case to hold in front of me!

Helen turned and did a vampish walk to the cheers and continued laughter of the customers. When she came into the back room she was flushed and she looked excited.

"Like what you saw, wee man," she drawled at me, then, seeing that I was embarrassed, she gave me a hug that nearly drowned me in cleavage. "If you were just a wee bit older.... But for the next few years you'll just have to be content with looking."

She buttoned her blouse, rolled her skirt down to its proper length and added: "Do you fancy a cuppa?"

Helen and I became great friends after that. She took me seriously and would try to answer my questions honestly. I had fancied girls but she was the first one I ever talked to as a person – I still have a crush on her!

There was only one question that she treated in an offhand way. I wanted to know what was so special about the 'special cream teas' but she would just giggle and tell me I was too young to understand. Even Uncle James, who always took me seriously, would only laugh and avoid giving me an answer.

You can imagine that finding out what was so special as to cause these strange reactions became an obsession with me. I never would have found out if it had not been for my Mum.

I love my Mum – it goes without saying, really – but my impressions of her are rather vague. She fusses me and always behaves as if I was still a wee baby; I sometimes think that she would like me to be an invalid so she could look after me and I would be totally dependent on her. She would not want me to be in pain or anything like that but just ill enough to need her constant attention. I react to her suffocating love by avoiding her when I can and ignoring her when I can't.

She used to read to me when I was little but since we moved to a new house in Whiteinch three years ago she seems to devote all her love to the house. She is always cleaning it, changing the curtains and getting my Dad to redecorate even when there isn't a mark on the wall. He is very patient with her, most of the time.

He really wanted her to come to the island to see how Gran had settled into her new life. Mum just wanted to stay at home and play with her wee house but this time he put his foot down. He over-rode her arguments until he finally lost patience and yelled at her. I thought for a moment that he was going to hit her! Times like that you can easily imagine that he must put the fear of God into criminals.

Anyway, he got my Mum to visit the island, though only for one week. It was as a result of this visit that I finally learned about the special cream teas. My Mum does not really have a loud voice but it is penetrating

– you cannot ignore it, and I have tried, believe me!

Two things more set the scene. Mum has it in her mind that Gran is going deaf, mostly because she is an old lady. Nothing anyone can say will stop Mum talking much louder when Gran is about. The day that she arrived for the visit, I was at the back of the tearoom repairing the awning that was always being damaged by the wind. It was a warm evening and the back door was open.

"Well, Mother, I hear that your tearoom is a big success." She always called Gran 'Mother' although she was Dad's Mother not hers.

I could not hear what Gran said in reply in her soft Highland accent. The pair of them went into the main area for I could still hear my Mother's voice although I could not make out the words. I was not at all interested in their conversation and I went on fixing the awning. I had put the ladder away and was approaching the back door to wash my hands and scrounge a cake or two when I heard the swish of the beaded curtain.

"Is Effie still suffering from her little problem," my Mother asked, quietly for her although her penetrating voice was still clearly audible.

Gran said something in reply that I missed since I was still two or three paces from the door.

"Oh that's wonderful," shrieked my Mother. "Did the doctor give her pills to dry up the milk?"

"Not at all," replied Gran. "I just milk her twice a day like you would a cow."

"That's disgusting. I can't believe you would do that."

"It's not disgusting at all. Effie's milk is rich and very creamy. We have been using it right from the beginning in our special cream teas. The customers can't get enough of it! That scone you just demolished had Effie's cream on it!

"As a matter of fact I'm thinkin' of sending James across to the boffins with my own hair-brush."

Chapter Four: *Foresight May Be Vain*

My Gran planned her tearoom like a top secret military operation. As little as possible was committed to paper and she only confided on a 'need to know' basis. She had to tell the plumbers and electricians what she wanted and where it had to be put, of course, but that was the reluctant extent of her confidences.

Even Aunt Effie, who was notionally her equal partner, had to ask Uncle James what he thought his sister had planned.

"Old movies," was his opinion. "She's always been daft about old black and white films with the likes of Ronald Coleman or Claudette Colbert. Remember when we were kids there was a man who trailed his projector and portable screen round the Highlands and Islands in his wee van showed nothing else but films that were twenty years out of date.

"I mind once Cissie and me went to Inverness to a proper cinema: it was magic, with Sean Connery as James Bond, but she just sniffed and said she preferred Douglas Fairbanks.

"She'll have planned the tearoom to look like the set for Casablanca – you mark my words!"

He was on the right track but had taken a wee detour. What Gran had in mind was a Parisian bistro. She had always fancied sitting on a stool at the door, dressed in a long black frock taking the money from the customers, while holding a cigarette holder made of jet or jade even although she has never smoked in her life! I think she would have brought back smoking in public just to recreate the ambiance!

When she bought the flat, the shop was an unexpected extra and she talked at first of making it into a sitting room until, that is, James told her she would look like one of the women on the Reeperbahn in Hamburg. He later explained the dig to Effie: Gran, I was surprised to note, laughed at his sally, clearly needing no enlightenment! Nobody bothered to explain it to me but I looked it up on the internet at school while the teacher was chatting up the classroom assistant.

An earlier owner with ambitions to introduce gracious cuisine to the island had fitted an expensive, stainless steel kitchen in an extension at the back of the original shop but he had run out of money before he had rewired the place. The plumbing was more than half done with water and drainage provided but no fitments. His plan for basic separate toilets for men and women was scrapped by Gran in favour of a plush uni-sex rest room with wee chairs and facilities for changing nappies.

The electrician fitted track lighting into the lost-wax moulding so it illuminated but remained unseen. Most of the moulding had survived since the building was constructed in the early years of the twentieth century and Hector Kitchen knew a man that could repair the damaged sections using vacuum formed plastic and plaster of Paris.

The lighting appeared to come from wall sconces that had already had a long record of service as swan-necked gas brackets. The electrician told me he had enjoyed converting them to electricity; when Gran handed them over to him they still had the wee knobs to turn on the gas and some of them even had the old mantles in place though most had crumbled into dust.

The fittings were elegant and looked very pretty with shades of scalloped ground glass etched with fruit and flowers. Gran had found them in a forgotten corner of a warehouse on Skye.

Henry Patel left his birthplace on the Indian Sub-continent at the age of eighteen. He had less than ten pounds cash and a vocabulary of about twenty words of English when he landed at Leith docks having worked his passage. Most of his wages from the voyage he sent back to his family with a note for his Mum saying the streets really were paved with gold. In fact, he had been miserably seasick for most of the voyage and he was appalled by the filthy streets surrounding the port.

He bought goods with his ten pounds, sold them at a modest profit and bought more goods. For the first year he survived on the charity of his more settled fellow countrymen, sleeping on their floors and sharing their food. He was a shrewd buyer and a persuasive seller so he slowly began to prosper. In his spare time he read library books to improve his English.

"I came to the Islands because of 'Kidnapped'," he told me.

"More likely he spotted an easy market amongst us ignorant Teuchters," Uncle James told me when he saw my romantic soul respond to this tale.

Whatever the reason, when Henry had turned his ten pounds into a thousand he took the train to Kyle of Lochalsh and crossed on the ferry to Skye where he negotiated good terms for the lease of an old byre. He stocked it with goods, bought a decrepit old van and started selling the very things that people wanted on their own doorsteps. He undercut the shops and was always cheerful. He would do his best to supply everything his customers needed so it did not take him many years to thrive mightily.

Having mastered English by reading the classics he became fluent in Gaelic. His only absence was a single trip home in his third year on the islands. He came back married to his childhood sweetheart. On his return, he rented a shop where his wife, who spoke only Hindi, presided with benign dignity. She spent most of the next ten years pregnant and thereafter looked pregnant even although she was not. Her English never did improve much but her happy smile and willingness to extend credit endeared her to the islanders.

His business, still based in Skye, had prospered deservedly and he was now a mighty pillar of the community. He made his home on our island after the birth of his second child because, he said, Skye was too crowded. (I think he must have included sheep in his census!) The day to day running of the business was now in the hands of his oldest children and sundry cousins who had appeared over the years but he was still cheerfully supplying the things people wanted at competitive prices leading, it appeared, a blameless life.

He had one weakness that he fondly imagined was a secret – at least from his wife! He could not resist a bargain and as the money rolled in he indulged his taste for the unusual and exotic by buying the most bizarre lots at auction sales all over the north and west of Scotland. He had kept the original byre he rented as his secret warehouse where he stashed the treasures he could not dare tell his wife he had bought.

"My dear wife would smite me if she knew that I had taken bread from the mouths of my children to buy what I can never hope to sell!" he told me when I visited this secret cache on Skye with Gran. His English tended to be a bit flowery, probably from using Scott and Stevenson as primers.

His youngest boy was at school with one of Gran's waitresses who told me that the whole family knew the secret, including his mum, about the store of rubbish and simply treated it as dad's hobby.

He had unearthed the gas fittings from the junk room of an auction house in Inverness, placed there when they had failed to reach their reserve so often that the owner lost all interest. Henry had bought them with a number of other unrecognised treasures after a seemingly cursory glance into the room.

He was a wonderful old schemer. He must have conned Gran into telling enough of her plans for him to make a shrewd guess at the things he owned that would appeal to her. I am sure that he changed things around in the warehouse before her visit so that the gas fittings would be unearthed by her as she rummaged. If he had shown them to her directly she would have been suspicious but letting her find them for herself piqued her interest.

When I went with her he used another well-worked ploy. He talked to her at length, and knowledgably, about old movies.

"I remember," he mused, "a film where the gestapo were in the street about to arrest the heroine when the old lady at her desk behind the till in the café pulled out a machine gun and shot the whole squad.

"Do you know, I think I have a till like that somewhere?"

It took him all of thirty seconds to produce a monstrosity. It stood about a metre high and was ornately decorated with pierced brass and scroll-work. I know for a fact that it had never left the British Isles for service in Paris because the operating keys, that were about the size of ten pence pieces, were engraved with pounds, shillings and pence. When you pressed a key, up popped a card with the amount printed on it into a glass compartment at the top that could be viewed from both sides of the counter.

Gran's eyes grew misty when she saw it and she even seemed to clutch an imaginary gun as she stood, rapt in the presence of this relic. Henry was a master: he said not another word but wandered off hardly noticing, it seemed, the effect his find was having. He came back after a few minutes to price it and take an end with me to load it in Gran's car less than thirty seconds later!

The original intention was to put the till in a booth at the door where she could have lived out her fantasy, but common sense reasserted itself when she realised that it would reduce the number of tables in the tearoom. She decided to load the till onto a trestle table just outside the kitchen that it shared with plates of cakes each protected by a transparent dome. This brought the glass window to a level where Gran could grin through it at the customers. The glass was old and a bit wavy so the effect of seeing Gran through it was a bit disconcerting since she appeared to be pulling grotesque faces when she moved like the distorting mirrors they used to have on fairgrounds.

Of course, the cards would have obscured her view but since many of them were missing and the currency had been abandoned years ago, this was no problem. Many of the keys did not function or had lost their knobs leaving a formidable spike to catch the unwary. One small key that did work was marked ¼. This represented a farthing, one quarter of an old penny or one nine hundred and fortieth of a pound. We are talking High Finance here!

The only key we were supposed to use was marked 'No Sale'. It took some force to move it but when it gave way with a little click, the cash drawer opened with a clatter. Transaction complete, the drawer was pushed shut where it was held in place by a catch that had become somewhat worn over the years. An incautious movement often led to it releasing the drawer. I was caught once or twice when I reached across the till to help myself to a cake and was rewarded by the sharp edges of the weighty cash drawer springing out to hit that part of me whose emptiness had prompted the attempted theft.

Every time the drawer sprung open it caused the trestle table to vibrate sending the plates of cakes under their neat little domes precessing towards the edge. Every 'No Sale' encouraged the cakes to edge towards the exit and we all got into the habit of pushing them back into place as we passed in or out of the kitchen. We got so good at it that I don't think we had a single disaster after the first month

Although the till opened unexpectedly it only did so when someone was touching it, but Gran began to worry that it would start opening under the very noses of customers admiring the cakes. She pictured their eyes widening in greed when they were confronted with a drawer full of cash presented to them in, it seemed, open invitation. At the same time, she stubbornly resisted any suggestion that she send the till to a museum and replace it with something more up to date – the 1980's perhaps!

She could not admit, even to herself, that she had saddled us with a monstrous liability.

Her solution was to take twenty pound notes out of the cash drawer and put them in a shoe box kept beneath the trestle table amongst boxes of doilies and paper napkins. She seemed oblivious to the fact that all the locals and many of the visitors knew not only what was in the box but also where it was stashed. Since the cache survived unrifled for the first year since the opening of the tearoom, Gran became smugly assured that she had found the perfect method to combat opportunist crime.

"It will certainly make my job a lot harder if it catches on in Glasgow," my Dad commented.

That first year had been a big success. Even during the off-season it was busy and when the tourists were about you usually had to queue for a table. When I arrived for the Easter holidays on the first anniversary of the grand opening, Gran asked me to do a trial balance of the books before she sent them to the accountant.

I had no knowledge of book-keeping but it was fairly straightforward to go through the till receipts and the box of invoices from suppliers. The cost of starting up had already been dealt with so I only had to look at the running costs. Gran had imposed a strict regime for recording the till takings in a hard-backed accounts book and she had matched all the bills with the cancelled cheques used to pay them.

It took me a couple of hours to find that the business had been running at a whopping loss. I took rather longer to check that I had missed nothing but at the end of a day spent at a table in a corner of the tearoom, I had to tell Gran that she was losing money hand over fist.

She first went white, then red, jumping up and marching up and down the room swearing in Gaelic. She stopped long enough to more or less accuse me of lax arithmetic but she stopped when she saw my stricken face. Effie had been locking up when I told Gran and she was now standing looking bewildered. I explained about the disaster and she turned to Gran who gave her a savage look and nodded before again pacing the room still cursing.

I do not know enough Gaelic to be sure but I am absolutely certain in my own mind that she did not repeat herself once during the entire tirade!

Effie burst into tears and ran off home twisting her hands together as she went. A quarter of an hour later Uncle James let himself into the tearoom to find me still sitting at the table with the receipts in front of me and my head in my hands. He glanced at me then strode past Gran towards the kitchen door. He went behind the trestle table, bent down and pulled out the shoe box. Without saying a word, he brought the box over to me and turned it upside down onto the scraps of paper.

Out tumbled a cascade of twenty pound notes that had never been entered in the till receipts. In an instant the apparent loss became a handsome profit. James, still without having spoken, turned to the door with a look at his sister that could have sunk the Titanic.

Chapter Five: *The Guinea's Stamp*

Most of the people on the island are related: there is a noticeable lack of variety in surnames. Even Christian names are chosen from a limited short list since the custom of naming children after their grandparents persists. The most extreme case I heard of is identical twin boys both christened Peter – the eldest (by just over a minute) after the paternal grandfather and the younger after the maternal grandsire.

On rare occasions naming a child after his grandfather can be followed by more serious consequences. My young cousin was christened Farquhar for his mother's father (she married a lowlander who offered no contest) a name that passed without remark when he started school in the Renton. Things took a nastier turn, however when he went with his parents and younger brother as emigrants to Australia. The family rented a property at first and Farquhar went to the local secondary school. At fourteen he was an inch or two over six feet tall and years of shinty had left his body as hard as his soul. Nonetheless his name caused great hilarity to his new schoolmates and he was forced to defend his patrimony on an almost daily basis. When they moved to a permanent address he announced that he would be called 'Jim' when he changed schools.

"I don't mind it too much," he told me, his lilting voice already losing its distinctive accent. "It's just that my knuckles are getting awful sore – worse than getting hit by a caman!"

When you are in the throes of courting it is hard enough to remember to ask your lover's full name and address far less stop to consider the consequences of the names of grandparents. I only mention this because of a nasty personal experience. When I went into my last year in primary school there was a new girl in the class and I fell totally in love with her. Amazingly, she liked me and we used to meet every playtime at the back of the science room. Everything was going like a dream until the moment that I plucked up the courage to ask her to the pictures with a promise of undying love.

She burst into tears and ran away! Not the greatest boost to my ego, I have to admit. Turns out that her Dad was doing a course at the Uni and they were going back to Weymouth the very next week. I didn't even know where Weymouth was until I looked it up in the atlas. We promised to keep in touch by text and email, parting with tears on both sides. I had just learned about exponentials and our correspondence followed a classical exponential decay – fifty messages the first day dropping to none by the second week.

She had found another boy by that time. I was still faithful but only because the girl I fancied laughed when I declared my passion. So far, I have to say, adolescence is a bummer: I had much more fun before I discovered girls. My Dad says it doesn't get any better when you are older.

Certainly there is too much angst to take the time to enquire about relatives. It is only when the honeymoon is over and lust has faded to an odd twinge, like rheumatics only more fun, that practical considerations make themselves apparent; to give just one example: will she look like her mother in another twenty years?

Perhaps this is why we have more or less scrapped naming children after grandparents in the cities. How ridiculous, after all, to have twins named Peter when they could have proudly borne traditional Scottish names like Wayne or Tyrone. You know you are home when, strolling at dusk through the urban box canyons of Maryhill or Denniston, you hear the maternal chorus:

"Ho! Wayne! C'm on in, son. Ye'r tea's ready."

"Is your Clint still oot, Belle? So's ma Tyrone. See me, a'll skin him when a get hold of him!"

"C'mon and gi'e yer Mammy a wee kiss, Wayne."

"Give me a break, Mother, I'm a twenty-four year old chartered accountant!"

"You'll always be my wee wean, Wayne."

In the more refined parts of the British Isles the Peters might have been distinguished by tagging them 'major' and 'minor' but on the island they were given nicknames. Many of these derive from the occupation of the individual like Neil the Post or Iain the Pier.

When I hear people say that they are tracing their ancestry through the census or parish records, I often wonder how they might do it on the island: there is no register of nicknames, or of their relationship to the baptismal record. Government documents like the census or pension book are a necessary evil, an invasion of privacy that may be legal, even necessary, but not wholly welcome and certainly not in tune with the people.

The islanders know what they are doing although it may sometimes seem strange to outsiders. For example Neil the Post has been retired for a number of years now. The mail is now delivered by his son, Christened Lachlan but known by everyone as 'Young Neil' or 'Neilac'. His friends from school have always called him Neilac and even his wife does – at least when they are in company. (She has a fine voice so we know of several other epithets she uses despite the metre-thick walls of their croft house.)

My Uncle James was called 'Philip' by everyone on the island. It came about in this way: in Gaelic, James is Seamus; in the United States a shamus is a private detective; the best known private eye when James was young was Philip Marlowe; simple, really!

The custom of soubriquets is so pervasive that strangers are often totally unaware of the given name. I was down at the boat one day when the Laird scrunched onto the shingle.

"Is Philip about?" he asked looking me up and down since it was the first time he had met me. I later saw him give the same measuring look to a tup he was thinking of bidding for.

"Uncle James," I yelled expecting that he would hear me in the byre where he was mending creels.

"Will your Uncle James know where Philip is?"

It turned out that he wanted my uncle to take a friend of his up to the lochan behind the croft where there were some well-grown trout.

"He's a Lord, don't ye know," added the Laird. "So look after the chap – see he gets into a couple of nice fish."

The Lord arrived later in the mandatory Range Rover from which he extracted enough gear to mount a trans-Andean expedition. He was tall, spare and slightly stooped; his military air was so pronounced that it was hard not to come to attention and salute.

"A very nice man, with no side to him," the Laird had assured us. He shook Uncle James by the hand just as if they were equals, as he looked him over from wellingtons to flat cap. I seemed to be somewhere below his radar: he neither looked at me nor talked to me during the whole evening!

"No need for formalities here, Philips. All lads together, what? No need for you to call me 'your Lordship' all the time – just call me 'sir'".

Having established his credentials as a man of the people, equitable to a fault, he strode off leaving James and me to carry all the gear.

The evening was a mixed success. The midges were out in force so the Lord, being a non-smoker, was in great discomfort. On the other hand, the trout were equally irritated and snapped intemperately at the fly specially selected by Uncle James. The Lord had been inclined to dispute the choice of lure at first since he had brought a selection of flies prepared for him "by a little man in London who has a wonderful understanding of these things."

In the end, after a barren half-hour, he bowed to local knowledge so we were able to net three nice trout, one of them more than two pounds in weight.

The Laird met us and whisked us off for a celebratory drink. I was sent to the kitchen where I was royally treated to ginger beer and ham sandwiches with lashings of mustard. In the gun room, James was supplied with beer, which he loathes, while the Lord and the Laird made inroads into a bottle of good claret that he would have appreciated.

"I feel sorry for the Laird," James told me on the way home. "These incomers think they are doing him a favour by landing on him expecting to be entertained. It would have cost the noble Lord hundreds if he had paid full whack for the hire of the water and an experienced gillie but I'll bet he hasn't even given the Laird a bottle of whisky.

"It was excruciating to watch the Laird trying to find a topic of conversation that would spark a response. He finally hit on the key: money!"

"Philip takes a bit of an interest in the Stock Exchange, you know." The Laird is always keen to point out the best features of his livestock, whether cattle or crofters.

"Does he indeed," replied the visitor, smiling vaguely then turning his back on James. "Well, gold's the thing. Best hedge there is against recession. Never go wrong with gold. Just been on to my broker to buy: he gave me a good deal – almost insider trading, I'm almost ashamed to admit. You should get into gold, Henry," he enjoined the Laird.

The Laird winked at my Uncle, who put down his barely tasted drink and prepared to leave. The Lord fumbled about in his purse and finally produced a rather crumpled ten pound note.

"Thank you, your Lordship. It is very generous you are sir. Would you be wanting change?"

The Laird had to have a coughing fit at this point to avoid laughing out loud.

On the way home, Uncle James told me that the Laird was chairman of an investment club that most of the locals belonged to. The meetings tended to be informal, conducted over a pint or a gate more often than not. Only that morning he had met Neilac, the treasurer, and James, the secretary, on the pier where they were waiting for the boat to arrive.

Taking advantage of the chance meeting the three office bearers had agreed to sell the gold and gold-mining shares they had bought some months before. They considered that, with the recession easing, gold prices would fall and that they should reinvest in oil shares as the most likely to rise when the economy started moving.

The club had made more than ten thousand pounds on their gold trading, a return of just under forty per cent.

"Thank God for ignoramuses like his Lordship," Uncle James grinned at me. "If it wasn't for the likes of him buying when sensible men are selling us poor crofters would all be much poorer still!

"I used to worry about the people who lost money when we made a big profit. I thought they would be a lot like us investing their hard-earned savings. Now that I have met the noble Lord I can sleep easier.

"He thinks he has put one over on the benighted peasantry and we have profited by his folly so we are all tolerably happy. Even you got a belly full of food and ginger beer!"

Chapter Six: *Ghost Story*

"Do you believe in ghosts?" I asked Uncle James while we were repairing the lobster pots that had been damaged in the spring storms.

"Irrelevant!" was his only reply.

After a minute or two he stopped knotting the tarred string we were using, reamed out his old pipe then loaded it with a fresh charge of St Bruno flake. He took off his battered cap and held it around the bowl to keep out the wind so he could light up. When it was drawing nicely he put his cap back on hiding the gleaming white forehead above his weather beaten face: seeing my uncle outdoors without his cap was about as usual as seeing the Queen opening a new hospital in her nightie.

His face is nut-brown from constant exposure to the weather but, hidden by his flat cap, is an expanse of snowy forehead extending almost to the crown of his head which is surrounded by a halo of fine, silver hair.

"The thing is, ghosts exist whether I believe in them or not."

I had been reading M.R. James and I thought I was pretty clued up about ghosts.

"Aye, like enough the man knew about English ghosts but our island ghosts are a more homely lot: I never heard of one that did a' body harm. Tam O'Shanter, I suppose, had a wee bit bother but it sounded more playful than malicious. Maybe the lass with the cutty sark was bashful about her legs! It would be hard to predict how a spirit might react to personal remarks. I suppose they would be more accustomed to criticism than admiration of their bodily parts."

Uncle James knows perfectly well that Tam O'Shanter met a coven of witches, so why did he introduce the topic into a discussion on ghosts?

When my Gran brought me to the island at first, this sort of surreal conversation had me thinking the place was a cross between a nature reserve and an outdoor lunatic asylum. Now I had learned to wait for the underlying logic to keek out. Talking to the islanders is a bit like playing hide-and-seek with a five year old: he wants to hide but he needs you to keep interested so he shows you glimpses of a trailing foot or an elevated bum.

Elliptical, is the usual description of the debating style of the islanders but that is too simple a conic section. Maybe a hyperbolic parabola (a saddle shape, in case you are wondering) would fit the bill. The information does not come at you head-on or even from the side but sort of twines around you the way morning mist will when the sun starts to lift it.

"So no clanking chains for island ghosts?"

"Not at all. For one thing there was very little iron to spare on the island. Then again many of the restless spirits were the result of drownings and I never heard of seaweed clanking, though it will pop and crackle when it is dry."

We were sitting with our backs against the byre, the creels forgotten, James smoking contentedly while I was digging up piggy nuts at the root of the cow parsley – very tasty but gritty because you could never get all the dirt off them.

"Not that I have seen a ghost myself," he continued after a time. "But I have heard them more than once."

"Groans and popping seaweed, I suppose."

"Not at all, not at all. When my Father was concentrating hard – when he was busy with the accounts and such like – he had a habit of clicking his fingers. After he died, I sometimes hear that same sound."

"But that could have been anything – a twig tapping on the window, for example."

"True enough." He paused to get his pipe drawing well. "It just seems strange that the twig should only tap when I needed reminding of a chore that I had forgotten."

He just nodded when I suggested: "Your conscience, perhaps?"

"Ah well, it makes cowards of us all, as that manny Shakespeare said.

"My Grandfather could see ghosts. In fact he was with me when I heard my first ghost. I was about your age and *seanair* and me were carrying hay down the croft to the byre when I heard the dirge the undertaker chants when he leads the hearse to the cemetery. There was no one in sight except old Alasdair beag earthing up tatties on the next croft.

"My Grandfather dropped the hay he was carrying, doffed his cap and signalled me to do the same. Then the pair of us stood with heads bowed for a couple of minutes. 'Ah well,' said my *seanair*, 'that's Alasdair beag gone to his just reward.'"

"But I thought you said he was earthing potatoes?"

"So he was, but he died the next day and a week later, at just that time, his cortege passed the very spot where we had stood in silent reverence."

"If he was alive when you had the experience you can hardly describe him as a ghost, can you?"

"I would never be so presumptuous as to set limits to ghostly behaviour!

"What we do have on the island, and a damned nuisance they can be too, is kelpies."

"They're a sort of sea monster that steals babies, aren't they?"

"Nothing so crude or ill-mannered, I can tell you, and all the more dangerous for that. They use charm and persuasion to entice their victims. You never hear any complaints from folks that have been taken by kelpies – their families often are very displeased, mind you, since the victim is usually away for years and years. They come home, I have heard, looking not a day older than when they were taken. They must just age quickly once they're back, I think, since I could never see anything different about them myself!"

"How do you know it was kelpies that took them – they might just have gone off with a party of tourists for a wee look at the real world?"

"Dear me. Is that what you would call being away with the fairies?"

We sat quietly for a time. James had knocked the dottle out of his pipe and he was sitting softly humming a Gaelic song.

"Do you think the witches on your island would dance at midnight in a ruined church?" I mused, expecting that my uncle would dodge the question since he was inclined to be defensive about the secret government magic laboratory that the villagers supplied with provisions.

"Ah well! There's one or two yonder," he replied, pointing the stem of his pipe towards the little island just beyond the mouth of the harbour, "that certainly have the hurdies for it!

"Cissie, your Gran, was a bonnie dancer when she was a lass, you know. She often won prizes at the Highland Gatherings. Mind you, she was never one for cavorting in her sark so I would be just unable to give an opinion on the state of her hurdies."

Later. I asked her about her career as a dancer, but she just chased me out to fix the awning over the outdoor tables for, maybe, the hundredth time. Effie had heard my question and I could hear the smile in her voice as she turned to Gran as soon as I was out the door.

"It was those knickers with the lacy frills round the legs that you used to wear that won you all the prizes. You weren't anything special as a dancer! I was only a wee lassie at the time but, oh my, how I envied you your frilly drawers. "

"Aye, true enough. I fairly made the judges sit on the edges of their seats so they could get a proper view – maybe I should call it an improper view. It was a good job my father was involved in judging the pipe bands: if he had spotted those knickers he would have cut my legs off!

"As for James, he never missed a chance to ogle my hurdies even although he is my brother. Imagine him telling the lad he never looked!"

Chapter Seven: *White Settlers*

People come to the island from all corners of the globe. Most of them simply visit, enjoy the tranquillity and the views, and then go home. Many of them return again and again and a number of them fall in love with the place and decide to stay. There are all sorts of reasons for moving to a new home: some come to work as teachers, doctors, local government officers and so on. The natives are friendly and welcoming although more restrained than, let's say, the residents of Hawaii – you are out of luck if you expect my Uncle James to put a lei around your neck as you step off the ferry!

There are a mercifully small number of visitors who decide to take up residence in the misguided belief that the island is nirvana and that the islanders have mastered some universal truth that enables them to live contentedly in the twenty-first century.

Shangri La with added midges, you might call it.

Uncle James thinks that the mastery they detect in the islanders is simply a thrawn unwillingness to engage with modern reality.

"They have their i-televisions and plasma-phones," he mused. "We have very little need of such sophistication. Mind you, I have heard them talking on their mobile contraptions and they seem to say a great deal about nothing at all so perhaps they need them less than they think.

"Modern communications are wonderful but I do not believe that we have the human skills to match the technology. I hear, for instance, that there are fortunes to be made switching money at high speed all over the world. I like to keep my cash in my pocket at least until the coins have reached body temperature."

The islanders would feel perfectly happy to watch the White Settlers, as the nirvana seekers are called, if they in turn would do the same – at least until they better understood what it was that made the island life so attractive. The incomers are a bit like animals born and raised in a zoo that need to be trained to survive in the wild before they are set free.

The natives belong to the land, conscious that their individual tenure is short. Most of them hold their crofts under the Crofting Acts that give them unshakeable tenure and strictly controlled rents. They are not great joiners so the newcomers soon find places on local councils and committees.

"Someone has to run things," they argue, ignoring the fact that they moved to the island because of the attitude of the natives. No sooner are they in positions of influence than they start improving on the perfection that attracted them in the first place.

Tranquillity away from the pollution of noise and light may be what they sought but they are soon petitioning to have street lights installed!

There is a well maintained but totally unnecessary road on the island that is called the Committee Road (pronounced 'commie-tee') since it was voted through by a committee largely composed of incomers. It was supposed to have a cattle-grid but one of the islanders on the planning group quietly arranged to have it fitted to the entry to his croft to save him the expense of putting in a gate!

Incomers are often aggressively 'green' with a sincere wish to save the planet. The natives are relentlessly practical: it makes sense to them to use an old bedstead for a gate, with baling wire to fasten it in place, but the incomers find it unsightly. Peat is a useful fuel and cutting it gives healthy exercise but, of course, it is far from smokeless. The fact that peat reek is an aromatic enhancement of the beauty of the views is overlooked.

White Settlers can become agitated when they are thwarted,

believing that the natives are reactionary idiots. The islanders think the incomers are hasty and will likely improve by the third or fourth generation.

My second cousin is a builder on the island (to tell the truth, he is the only builder) and he was asked to build a house for an incoming settler from Hampshire. He has worked around Glasgow: indeed he brought his bride back from Lanark. She was a nursing sister and took a job in the cottage hospital; one of the first things she did was to learn Gaelic so that she could comfort the old patients who forgot their English *in extremis*.

"Here are the plans, Angus," the client began. "It is a partly pre-fabricated design as you can see."

"A very fine house indeed and I can certainly put it up for you. There don't seem to be any outbuildings shown on the plan: you will surely be building a byre?"

The accountant laughed heartily and you could see him storing the tale away to regale his cronies at his golf club in the Home Counties.

"No byre, but I might put in a gazebo later."

"For myself, I would favour a zareba."

Price and timescale were swiftly settled although it would be fair to say that the completion date, firm in the opinion of the accountant, was more of a work in progress to my cousin.

All was going wonderfully well until they visited the site and the client showed the plot he had marked out.

"I can't build it there," said Angus.

"If you won't I will find someone else who will," replied the accountant, stomping off in the highest dudgeon. Angus was left trying to explain his objections but a soft-spoken islander is no match for an irate Englishman.

He found a Glasgow firm that was prepared to build it wherever he told them to. The cost was slightly higher but the customer was well-satisfied to have put a native in his proper place.

"I tried to explain why it was impossible," Angus told James. "I even tried to show him one or two places that would have done not far away but he would not be told."

Construction began in March and the timber-framed dwelling was ready for occupation by October.

"You said it couldn't be done," the accountant crowed when he met Angus outside the bank at the beginning of November.

"I said it shouldn't be built there."

"Whatever. It's standing there now ready for me to move in."

It was still standing at the end of February but in March the equinoctial gales whipped the roof off and flattened the gable wall.

"I tried to explain that the Gaelic name for the site was the four winds: the hills act just like a wind tunnel. Ach, White Settlers!" Angus spat into the harbour where we sat watching the accountant board the midday ferry for his final journey back to England.

Fortunately not all the incomers are like that. Clifford, for example, is more like a native than many of the islanders – particularly the younger ones. He followed Marie bhan back from Swansea when she gave up being ward manager in a big hospital to be matron of the cottage hospital.

Clifford fitted in right from the start. He kept his Welsh accent but he was very easy going except when his homeland played rugby against Scotland. Not that the islanders are much bothered about sports other than shinty and football but Clifford could become provocatively boastful after the seemingly inevitable Welsh victory.

He was an enthusiastic toper with a guilt complex so a victory at rugby gave him a perfect reason to celebrate. Fortunately, he had a weak head so the lads he would drink with quickly got him drunk and carried him home to Marie before anyone could take offence at his triumphalism.

He was Welsh chapel and fitted in seamlessly with the rather austere form of Presbyterianism favoured on the island. He became the church organist and would gladly have been choirmaster too if the natives had been willing to tolerate the sinful frivolity of people singing in harmony.

Marie and he were well suited. A typical matron, she viewed life with a realistic if somewhat steely eye, keeping any compassion she felt well hidden from public view. Her one human weakness was a totally unfounded belief that Clifford was one of nature's total abstainers who would allow his good nature to be talked into having a small libation just to be sociable. Clifford loved her and tried to overcome his monumental appetite for alcohol to meet her expectations. Apart from rugby victories by the principality he would stay off the water of life for months.

The only thing that totally undid him was New Year. He would slip out on Hogmanay and tour the island, passing out from time to time but carrying on undaunted. He was in no danger for there was always someone to pick him up, clean him off and put him to bed. He would return to the warmth of his own fireside sometime before the tenth of January – most years.

Last year I was on the island over Christmas because my Mum thought I would have fewer distractions and could revise for my Highers prelims.

I was on the bus going back to the croft on the fifth of January with Clifford, well fuelled and a good deal dishevelled, as the only other passenger. He was snoring quietly when the driver pulled up at his road end and asked me if I would see Clifford the last hundred metres to his front door. The driver could not wait because he had to pick up the mail from the ferry.

Clifford woke up merry and voluble but had to be carefully steered to keep him out of the ditches that bordered the track. Where older and wiser heads would have left him inside his gate, I took him all the way and propped him up while I rang the bell.

"*Co tha sin?*"

"I just brought Mr. .. Clifford, home."

At the precise moment that Marie opened the door, Clifford was extravagantly sick all over the doorstep and up Marie's legs to the knees. The usual heavy miasma of vomit was almost lost in the alcohol fumes arising from the multi-coloured puddle.

"Oh Clifford," she said, helping him across the threshold. Then she turned to me.

"Thank you. I expect someone gave him a chocolate. Clifford has a very delicate stomach and chocolates always make him sick."

Chapter Eight: *Droit de Segnioure*

It was the Laird who won me my chance to go to university. I had worked hard and I was predicted to get good results in my Highers. Mathematics and physics were my best subjects but I was also expected to do well in English and Geography. My worst subject was languages: my French was just appalling. I felt ill at ease with a tongue that ascribed masculinity to inanimate objects – a bit like that big centre back my team signed last season!

University had been talked about in our house from time to time but with the Prelims just weeks away the discussion intensified.

"The bottom line then is this:" (my Dad had recently picked a few phrases of that sort, usually ones that had gone out of circulation years ago!) "On the one hand, you go to university, costing us several thousands, and at the end there is no guarantee of a job. On the other hand, you become articled to a Chartered Accountant, get a small wage while you are training and finish up with a licence to print money."

He paused and my Mum and I waited while he smirked before he launched the punch line: "That's what we call a never-minder!"

"I think you mean a 'no brainer', dear," my Mum interjected.

"Whatever: accountancy here you come."

If you have ever argued with your Dad you will know how difficult it is. I have never developed a technique that even got me a hearing – he just ignored me.

In school I took the application forms for Glasgow University to avoid having to explain myself in front of the whole class but I went to see my form teacher after school to return the documents. I broke down in tears as if I was seven instead of seventeen and she started crying along with me! I had to plead with her not to telephone my Dad there and then.

Next day I was summoned to the Headmaster's office where he put the blame squarely on me!

"Stand up for yourself, boy. Are you a man or a mouse?" He went on in the same vein for the best part of an hour but at least it was during my French lesson so it was not all bad!

The atmosphere remained tense both in school and at home until the Christmas holidays. Dad must have been feeling a bit guilty because he took a few days off work so he and I could go to the island.

"We'll leave your Mother and the wee ones to decorate the tree and all that while you and me go and do a bit of male bonding."

On the way north, he explained that his new Chief Inspector was a graduate: "A right sumph, I can tell you!" (I could not help wondering if the new-comer was the source of the out-dated mid-Atlantic slang that had crept into Dad's vocabulary.)

"We won't bother your Uncle James and Aunt Effie with our family problems," he warned me as we boarded the ferry. But on the island secrets evaporate like mist on a summer morning: neither of us said anything about the decision on my future although James and I had discussed it at length during the summer.

Effie gave me a big hug and called me 'a wee lamb' and even Uncle James punched me on the shoulder and gave me a wink so I guess that my face must have shown them that all was not well. Even Inspector Clouseau could have figured out the reason for my misery so it was easy for Uncle 'Philip Marlow' James!

The morning after we arrived, the Laird turned up with his estate manager and a couple of rifles. He easily convinced Dad to join him to hunt a lone stag that had got into the recently planted forest, either over or through the deer fence, and was eating its way through the saplings. The topmost shoot is a particular delicacy and its removal can set back the growth of the tree by three or four years.

Uncle James and I went down to the shore and filled a couple of bags with whelks in companionable silence. Dad was very quiet when he got back from the hunt and he spent the next day on a solitary walk to the lochan behind the croft.

When we were in the car going home, with a haunch of venison in the boot, he pulled into a lay-by, switched off the engine and turned to face me.

"You'll be going to university after all." I was stunned into silence. For some minutes there was no sound but the ticking of the cooling engine. Dad was still looking at me and I was trying to find some words – any words – that would show my surprise, gratitude, not to mention the fear that I would make a mess of my Highers. Suddenly he thumped both hands on the steering wheel and grinned at me.

"The Laird gave me a right telling-off after we had killed the stag: 'University is not an upmarket job centre,' was his opening salvo. He went on to talk about opening your mind to new ideas, widening your horizons. 'The lad deserves his chance.' He said a lot more along the same lines but that's the gist of it. He had me squirming, I can tell you: the last person to talk to me like that was my old Headmaster, and that wasn't yesterday!"

It is strange how coincidences happen in real life. When we arrived home we stepped out the car into the path of my form teacher who was clearly on her way to our house. When she saw us she stopped and hopped from foot to foot. When she turned to me her face was bright scarlet.

"I know you made me promise not to say anything but I really, really believe that university is the proper place for you." She turned to Dad but before she could open her mouth he said: "I agree – I was a fool ever to think otherwise. Thank you for caring enough to come here. Will you come in for a wee refreshment since it's nearly Christmas?"

When I telephoned James to tell him he just gave me the Laird's phone number and told me to thank him myself. I thought that the man had not even noticed me: Uncle James just laughed.

"He misses nothing that goes on. Like it or not, you are one of his men now and he always looks after his own."

When I finally plucked up the courage to telephone the big house, the Laird answered and recognised my voice!

When I went to the island at Easter, with good results in my Prelims (even French!) and a provisional place at Glasgow University, I wanted to know all about the Laird: he was my new hero!

I thought that he had been born and bred in the big house but it turned out that he had only been on the island for about ten years. Before that he had been a barrister, living in London, specialising in company law. He took a leave of absence when his father had a stroke and stayed on when the old man died a few months later.

"But you must have known him when he was growing up here," I insisted.

"His father only bought the estate in 1956 when he retired from the army."

He had been the Colonel of an infantry regiment and his only connection with the Highlands of Scotland was a romantic notion he had conceived from the stories of Robert Louis Stevenson and Sir Walter Scott that he relaxed with when campaigning with his troops!

Nothing daunted the Colonel, and he bull-dozed his way through obstacles whether they were created by reactionary crofters or intransigent officials of local or central government. Crofts are held under a very special rental arrangement supervised by a Commission in Edinburgh. The tenure of a croft is secure and heritable while the rents are vanishingly low.

The Colonel might battle to the death with officialdom but he accepted with equanimity the rights of his hard-working tenants. He soon decided to make a ceremony of the half-yearly rent collection, going from croft to croft giving a dram to the men and Hermes scarves to the women – spending more than he collected by a substantial margin. He even tried his hand at learning Gaelic.

A poor ear for language and a great fondness for whisky resulted one year in a nine days wonder that was extended, by popular demand, to a fortnight!

The Colonel had lost his licence despite the best efforts of his friends on the Magistrates bench. (It was rumoured that the Chief Constable had threatened to go to the Daily Record if they acquitted him again.) He overcame this obstacle by bullying his housekeeper into chauffeuring him around the crofts.

He was a dapper little man, slim, beautifully dressed and with a neatly trimmed military moustache; the housekeeper, in contrast, was large, lumpy, with greasy hair and foods stains making a dot-to-dot of her bobbled twin sets.

All would have been well if the Colonel had stuck to his native tongue but he had made up his mind to conduct all his business in Gaelic. Sadly a few lapses in vocabulary and grammar meant that his attempts to explain that his housekeeper was simply driving him around translated into an announcement that he had proposed marriage to her and had been accepted.

She did not know a word of the language so she just sat there nodding and smiling while the Colonel ploughed on. The islanders were too polite, and far too surprised, to do more than mumble a few words of congratulation. The misunderstanding continued until the Minister called at the big house to discuss the publication of the banns. I would like to have been a fly on the wall when that revelation unfolded!

The Colonel always claimed that running the estate was just the same as running a regiment.

"Make sure the women and children are well cared for if you want to get the best out of the men."

By all accounts he worshipped the men of his regiment, spoiled the kids and admired the ladies. He was always a perfect gentleman but he missed no opportunity to put a comforting arm around a shoulder or plant a bristly kiss on a fair cheek. That is why the islanders were not too surprised when he seemed to be engaged to his housekeeper.

There things would have stopped had it not been for the visit of the Colonel's old Adjutant.

"He was a really nice man," Uncle James told me. "Eton and Sandhurst and a bit of a debutantes delight in his youth, at least according to him! Tall and distinguished looking with his hair, greying at the temples, kept well in check – probably with Brylcreem."

James took him fishing on a dull, overcast day when there was little chance that any fish would rise. My uncle always took a flask of whisky with him 'for medicinal purposes' and the Major had done the same. What with the lack of fish, the rawness of the day and compatible temperaments the medical needs were invoked to the point where the old soldier was three parts drunk.

"It's difficult to judge the dosage when you don't know someone well," as James explained to the Colonel when he poured his guest through the door of the big house.

Fortunately the Major was an amiable drunk – and an indiscreetly talkative one! Uncle James asked how the Colonel's policy of caring for the women and children of the regiment had worked.

"Only too well sometimes," the adjutant began. His tale was a bit rambling including names and dates with frequent stops to ponder whether things happened in April or the month before; since the events had taken place twenty years earlier such accuracy hardly seemed to matter.

The regiment was responsible for guarding the Falkland Islands long before they became a bone of contention between Britain and the Argentine. A subaltern with an experienced sergeant and twenty men spent a mostly tedious two years trying to keep out of trouble.

Sometime early in 1950 – 'April, it was: no, I tell a lie, it was June, or was it July' – a newly married officer was posted to the Falklands leaving his new wife in married quarters. "She was a big girl, not beautiful exactly but she had a wonderful seat on a horse. Her father was a baronet, the younger son of a duke, and she had been presented at court the previous year – 'coming out' we call it."

"It was a sort of upper class dating service," Uncle James explained to me. "The girls had a debutant season where they went to balls and parties and finished up going to Buckingham Palace to be presented to the King and Queen. Expensive, no doubt, but it gave lots of pleasure to the women of Britain who followed the season in the illustrated magazines. Harmless fun, really."

The abandoned bride had been brought up to believe that duty came first so she accepted the absence of her husband with good grace. The real trouble was that she did not get on any too well with the wives of the other officers. She was the youngest but that mattered less than the fact that her groom was the most junior officer in the regiment. She, as became the granddaughter of a duke, considered herself the natural leader of the wives and tried to condescend even to the wives of senior officers.

The Colonel was a widower and he was inclined to dismiss the unrest amongst the wives as a storm in a teacup when it was reported to him. As he always did when husbands were posted away on duty he went to visit the girl in her new home. Because of the unrest he spent rather longer there than was his custom.

Things settled down: the wives were polite to the cuckoo in the nest at official functions where the Colonel was likely to attend and quietly ostracised her for the rest of the time. It is doubtful if the former debutant even noticed.

When the Falklands posting came to an end the Colonel sprang a surprise. He changed the sergeant and soldiers but he left the officer out there with the sweetener of promotion. A few eyebrows were raised but the Falklands posting was less than popular so even the two senior subalterns did not grudge their young colleague his advancement.

So when four long years of separation finally ended there must have been rejoicing and tears of happiness? Not entirely: the problem was that his wife presented him with a bouncing baby boy only eighteen months old.

Accusations of infidelity were stoutly denied. "I was faithful all the time you were away. He is a true son of the regiment." In response to any further questioning she would burst into tears. When she recovered she repeated her mantra. She would not admit infidelity and simply reiterated her fidelity to the regiment.

Even the fairly dim lieutenant had by this time worked out that the father of the child was likely to be a brother officer. He became a nuisance in the mess, staring intently at his fellows then surreptitiously looking at a photograph of the infant to see if he could spot a resemblance.

Uncharacteristically the Colonel let this go on for some time. Indeed it became noticeable that he usually found some excuse to leave when the young man came in. When a meeting was unavoidable he developed a habit of tucking his head into his shoulder like a bad actor playing the hunchback of Notre Dame, effectively hiding his face.

Eventually everything has to be faced. The Colonel had, after all faced German storm troops and Pathans without flinching. He called the officer into his office for a 'chat'.

"Sit down my boy. I'm delighted to have you back. The regiment needs fine young officers like you – and that fine young boy you have, when he grows up, of course.

"Matter of fact it's about the boy that I want to talk to you. I understand that you are a bit worried that you were away for four years and he is only eighteen months old – longish gestation period, don't you know."

The lieutenant was sitting forward in his chair on the point of interrupting but the Colonel was too old and wily a campaigner to be forced into a discussion: he had a speech to make and make it he would using a gag if necessary.

"I talked the matter over at length with the Medical Officer. Bit of a poser for him but he went away and looked up some obscure text books and finally hit on the answer."

He picked up a piece of paper from the desk, adjusted his reading glasses and cleared his throat a couple of times.

"Let's see. Ah yes it is what the doctor calls a 'Vindictive Pregnancy'."

Still baffled the young man went straight from the Colonel's office to the Medical Officer, a Major who had been with the regiment even longer than the Colonel.

"Ay, I told the Colonel that it was a 'Vindictive Pregnancy'."

"But what does it mean? Can you explain it to me in layman's language?"

"Of course, of course: it means that someone had it in for you while you were away."

Chapter Nine: *Master and Lieutenant* *Commander*

"Did you ever go to the Falkland Islands when you were in the Navy?" I asked my Uncle James.

Before I even met him, my Gran had told me about her big brother who had been a heroic naval officer in 'The War'. According to her he had commanded a destroyer if not a cruiser. Ever since I had met him I had been trying to get him to tell me about his illustrious career without the least success.

Even a direct question was ignored. He would stand with a far-away look in his eyes and start humming a Gaelic song under his breath. If the question was repeated he would snap out of his preoccupation and stride off: "No time for frivolities – you and me have work to do. Did you ..." and he would pick unerringly on the chore I had not yet done.

When he did open up it seemed to be almost by chance. I was too young then to have mastered the elliptical approach to conversation favoured on the island. He had just been talking about the Laird's father when I asked James if he had ever been to the Falklands.

He was in the stern of the dinghy trawling two lines while I struggled to hold our position in the rip tide through the narrows. We were after lythe, a streamlined fish that favours fast flowing water that will bring food into its waiting jaws. It is not a difficult fish to catch if you can find where it is feeding: it snatches at the hook in the same way that it plucks sustenance from the tidal stream.

It is a pleasant enough occupation for the fisherman but it is hard, relentless toil for the rower. Uncle James had got the far-away look and had moved on from a rather mournful air to a much more cheerful waulking song after I questioned him about the Falklands. I dare say that I would have asked again and spoiled the moment if I had been able to find the breath.

We stayed until the ebb slackened and I was able to pull out of the easing current pleased with myself for holding our place for long enough to land three nice fish. James reeled in the lines, got his pipe filled and drawing to his satisfaction and then took over the rowing for the trip home.

"I have been to the Falkland Islands," he said at last. Then with a funny smile that looked more like a grimace of pain he added: "There was a wee bit of a War going on during my visit so my view of the place is rather limited!"

Before I could think of a response he went on.

"Your Grannie will have told you that I was a great hero, captain of a great ship of war – has she got me on the bridge of a battleship yet?"

I shook my head and he chuckled and continued.

"Give her time! A hard place, the Falklands, even more barren and windswept than the island if you can believe that! When I left school, I went down to Glasgow to the University to study agriculture." I must have shown my surprise because he laughed and deliberately missed his stroke to send a spray of icy water over me.

"Ay! You're not the only smart one in the family. I spent most of the four years at the campus in Ayrshire but I got to see the bright lights from time to time; especially in my final year when your Gran came down to start her nursing training. I used to pick her up from the residence on a Saturday night and we would saunter down to the Highlanders' Institute for a few drinks. Your Gran would be up for every dance but I mostly sat at the side enjoying the chance to speak Gaelic.

"Good times." He paused for a moment with the oars shipped while he got his pipe going again. The trouble was that I became infected by ideas. I used to come back to the croft every holiday to help my Father and I would be going on at him all the time about the improvements we could make to the productivity of our 'small-holding'. I mind the first time I called the croft a small-holding: we were mending a fences up near the fank and he threw a stob at me – missed me by about an inch!

"He and I fell to fighting most of the time: he hated my new-fangled ideas and I thought he was a dinosaur. I never thought of it until now but I have had the croft for fifteen years and I have never introduced a single one of the improvements I advocated so passionately.

"By the time I sat my final exams I was dreading coming back to the croft for good. My Father was very fit and likely to continue in charge for many more years. I gave the future a lot of thought. It would have felt like a betrayal if I had gone to work on another farm and I had no capital to set up a salmon farm – they were becoming all the rage at the time. So I opted for a diplomatic solution by joining the Royal Navy as a deck officer.

"The recruiting posters said 'Join the Navy and see the World.' I saw the Falkland Islands, a great deal of ocean and a fair bit of Whitehall!

"As a very junior officer hardly out of Dartmouth, I was appointed aide to an admiral. His name was Guthrie but he claimed direct descent from the Lords of the Isles. When he saw the name James Macdonald on the Navy List he called me in and made me his gopher.

"He was a lovely old man and he treated me like a nephew. He had some Gaelic learned mostly from gillies when he was boy and we spoke it when we were alone. He enjoyed malt whisky although he would only serve blended spirits to visitors. Looking back, my job was mostly keeping a supply of Talisker to hand – I even had a special pocket sewn into my uniforms to hold a half bottle!

"I remember one evening when we went in full dress uniforms to a dinner at an RAF base. We were being attended by a pilot officer who was even younger than me with the wings on his dress uniform so new they still glowed. Admiral Guthrie lit up a little cheroot while we waited in the anteroom for the call to the table.

"Blushing like a girl, our escort cleared his throat a couple of times, looked around and, catching the full force of a glare from his Group Captain, he leaned forward and confided to the admiral: 'It is the custom in the RAF not to smoke in the anteroom before dinner, Sir'. 'Custom,' bellowed the admiral, in whom discretion was a very thin veneer at the best of times, 'the RAF isn't old enough to have customs, my boy: it has habits and, so far as I can see, most of them are bad!'

"He finally let me return to the real Navy when a Macdonald from Barra became available. I was given my first, and as it turned out, my only active posting. I became First Lieutenant on a supply ship attached to the North Atlantic Fleet. It was a bit like Rory Cheese's travelling grocery but on a bigger scale. The skipper had the rank of Lieutenant Commander and he ran the ship in proper Naval fashion – there was no slacking on Her Majesty's Ship 'Ettrick Bay'!

"He was basically a good-hearted man but his bitterness over his failure to win promotion to Captain soured him. He treated the ship and crew – especially the First Lieutenant – as if she was the most vital cog in the whole machinery of the Admiralty; it was his way of showing their Lordships that he should have been commanding an aircraft carrier. I enjoyed it because, although he was demanding, he was fair; he was sparing with praise but we all glowed when he did bestow it.

"I had only been on board for a couple of months when the Argentinians invaded the Falkland Islands. We were sent into dock to be fitted with an anti-aircraft gun, filled with supplies including, prophetically as it turned out, body bags and joined a convoy to the South Atlantic.

"We anchored in a bay near the forward area and were soon rigged up as a field dressing station: doctors and nurses stabilised the wounds before the injured were moved to hospital. That's when we started using the body bags. We could hear the crump of artillery and we even heard the crackle of small-arms fire when the wind was in the right direction, but the only enemy troops we saw were on the fore-deck having their wounds dressed.

"That all changed at 0817 local time on a typical Falklands day. The wind was blowing up the inlet and had just pushed a heavy morning mist into the clouds that were so low you could not see the tops of the hills. I was on the bridge with the Captain going over the daily orders. We had a plan to modify the steam pipes to give some heating to the wounded and we had come up to the bridge so I could point out the details. The skipper knew he could have left it all to me but he always had to see for himself.

"We were wearing body armour and steel helmets – woe betide a crewman who put his nose out on deck without full protection! A yeoman came on deck and was standing close to the Captain waiting for us to finish talking. His presence had been acknowledged and he was standing looking over the rail waiting until his commanding officer was free to deal with him.

"He suddenly whispered 'Oh my God' and I looked up to see two Argentinian fighter jets just emerged from the cloud less than a mile away. I think the pilots were as surprised as we were for it took a moment for them to angle down towards us. As I watched there was a flash from the leading aircraft, bangs like a hammer hitting a bucket, then a wall of noise that battered the senses.

"I know now that only a second at most elapsed but it seemed like an age before my brain started working and I realised that we had been strafed. I was still looking out over the deck and I registered that nothing had been hit down there. I became aware that my cheek was wet and I remember thinking that a bullet must have hit a water pipe. I was wiping it away as I turned to the Captain.

"I did not understand what I saw: the yeoman had been on the far side of the skipper and he was now next to me, grey faced and in the act of falling to the deck. As my eyes followed him down I saw the captain spread-eagled on the deck with a bloody mask where his face had been. The hand that I had used to wipe my face was covered in blood and I stared at it in shock before focussing on the yeoman who was twitching and moaning with his left arm attached only by a ribbon of flesh and his ruined shoulder pulsing blood. I knew that I should be doing something about stopping the haemorrhage but my feet would not move.

"There's a bit in Shakespeare about all the perfumes of Arabia being unable to sweeten a bloody hand. For weeks and weeks I scrubbed my cheek raw where the skipper's blood had splashed me."

My Uncle and I talked all the time about anything and everything under the sun but this was by far the longest speech he had ever made. As he told it, his face had become more and more gaunt and most of the colour had drained from it leaving his weather-beaten cheeks blotched. He had stopped rowing at some time although I had not noticed when. Now he scrubbed his hand over his face, sighed and dipped the blades into the water. After no more than a dozen strokes, he shipped the oars again and started the ritual of cleaning, filling and lighting his pipe.

When it was drawing to his satisfaction he started rowing again with the slow, steady strokes that seemed to drive us through the water faster than my more enthusiastic efforts. I thought he would say no more but he surprised me again by going on, but in something much closer to his normal, rather ironic, delivery.

"So I got acting promotion in the field to Lieutenant Commander and became the Captain of HMS Ettrick Bay, eventually sailing her home and leaving the Royal Navy at the earliest possible opportunity."

"Do you think the Falklands War was a mistake? Surely we couldn't just have let the Argies take over, could we?"

"I have thought a lot about that over the years and read everything I could find on the subject and the result is the same: I do not know. Perhaps the politicians should have tried harder to find a solution but they didn't. I do know that a lot of money was spent and far too many men were killed or crippled.

"We forced the Argentinians off the Islands but they are still claiming them for themselves, still calling them the Malvinas. I often thought that you could have moved all the islanders with their livestock to the Ardnamurchan Peninsula for a fraction of the cost.

"You could have exhumed their forefathers, reburied them in Scotland, given their living descendants a pension for life and still come out on the right side of the balance sheet.

"They would even have benefitted from a gentler climate. The wonder to me is that anyone would want to stay on a barren, wind-swept desert far less two countries fighting for it.

"Mind you, I can't talk. People from the south don't think much of the climate on this island but I wouldn't swap it for a villa in Cannes and a generous pension. I like the fact that the weather changes from minute to minute – you have seen yourself how we can have all four seasons in a single day! I think my character has been formed by the land and the climate. I find it natural to get up at two in the morning to pick whelks at low tide. It seems right to go out only to tend to the beasts when the rain is lashing horizontally at windows bowing under the assault. So I appreciate why the Falklanders want to stay on their islands."

We had reached home and he paused while we pulled the boat above the high-tide mark and stowed the gear. Then he added, with a twinkle: "There have been days when that villa in France seemed very attractive. I mind thinking about it one day when I was standing chest deep in black peaty water trying to get a rope under the belly of a stirk too stupid to stay out of a bog...." But at that moment Aunt Effie came down to see what we had caught and I never did learn the fate of the brainless bovine.

Chapter Ten: *Wars Need Heroes*

Since I was about nine years old, my Gran had been telling me stories of her heroic wee brother commanding a ship of the line and winning medals in the war. When I met my Great Uncle James four years ago I was ready to hero-worship him but he flatly refused to indulge me by spinning me yarns about his daring. It was hard to understand why he would not talk about his military exploits: if it had been me I would have told everyone I met including total strangers walking past me in the street!

Uncle James and I had become great friends despite the difference in our ages – or, perhaps, because of the gap of fifty years. I was always asking leading questions but James was a past master at evasion. A faraway look and a Gaelic air hummed under his breath was all the answer he would deign to give.

Then, out of the blue, he told me on a fishing trip how he had been to the Falkland Islands during the war against Argentina. He had taken command of a supply vessel when her captain was killed by enemy aircraft fire. Not a cruiser, not even a frigate but a remarkable story that made Uncle James even more of an idol to me.

In fact, I felt a bit cheated that my Gran had found the need to embellish a tale that stood proudly on its own merits. Why would anyone gild something that was already solid gold? I lost very little time in telling her that I now knew the whole story.

"And did he show you his medals? You don't know even the half of the story, boy!"

Gran may not have read Clausewitz, although nothing about her would really surprise me, but she certainly shared the philosophy of Cleopatra: 'I will not be triumphed over.'

"I'll show you the medals, if you like, but before I do I must tell you the bits of the story that don't appear in the citations."

James and I were making up cardboard boxes from flat packs to ship the lobsters we were confidently expecting to land next morning. I should say that I was confident for my uncle was his usual unhurried, non-committal self.

"When I looked at the yeoman collapsing to the deck, my knees gave way and I fell, face down, bringing up my breakfast in painful retches. There was blood pumping from his shoulder and I knew that I should do something about it; I even remembered that I was trained in First Aid, but I couldn't bring to mind what it was I was supposed to do. I just lay there in my own vomit trying to make myself stand up and deal with the situation.

"It seemed like only seconds before I had recovered enough to try standing but it must have been longer for I was helped to my feet by a medical orderly who was using his other hand to explore my body for damage. The yeoman was still lying where he had fallen but a doctor and nurse were kneeling beside him and had stopped the bleeding. A second orderly was standing by with a stretcher, waiting until they had finished binding his shoulder.

"I stood gawping until they had finished, then the doctor came over and had a word with the orderly who was still helping me to stay upright. The doctor flashed a torch in my eyes as he held my chin with his other hand: 'You'll do', he said clapping me on the shoulder.

"So I assumed command of the ship before I was properly in command of myself. I sent a signal to the fleet reporting the attack and the death of the skipper, then I went the rounds to assess the damage to ship and crew on legs that needed stern control to stop them wobbling. The only physical damage was the single line of bullet holes slanting across the bridge and part of the after deck.

"The anti-aircraft gunners had been alert enough to fire at the jets as they raced overhead. It happened that they had been doing daily gun drill when the enemy appeared. I set them to counting the ammunition they had used after I had congratulated them.

"Two helicopters arrived just before noon. The first took out casualties from other skirmishes and our yeoman, and then the second helicopter landed a new lieutenant to take my place as First Officer and a rather sour looking Captain, Royal Artillery. The lieutenant RN handed me orders from the admiral: I was to command 'Ettrick Bay' with acting promotion to Lieutenant Commander - he even had the forethought to include a thin ribbon so I could add the half-stripe to my uniform.

"The Captain RA inspected the damage and our ammunition log. The bullets had started about an inch from where my head had been. When I saw how close a call I had had, my legs turned to jelly again and I had to hang onto the rail, trying to appear nonchalant, until a wave of dizziness passed.

"Our gunners had fired about five hundred shells but the artilleryman shook his head and told me that less than two hundred would have been anywhere near the target, 'unlikely though it is that half-trained naval gunners would get anywhere close to a barn door – even a stationery barn door!'

"The medical orderlies cleared the mess on the deck, the skipper went into one of his own body bags and I commanded all I surveyed. All that remained was to survive the Board of Enquiry."

"They couldn't blame you. You did everything you could!"

Uncle James smiled wryly. "You have a lot to learn about the official mind, especially the official military mind. There is a book covering all eventualities and it is more important to obey the instructions in the book than to do the job well. A Board of Enquiry always looks for the smallest deviation from Queen's Regulations so they can pillory some poor sod. The only safe way to avoid censure is to make a really big cock-up so they have to cover it up: but that is only used for admirals and above!"

James got his pipe drawing smoothly with a sort of contented gurgle much like the noise of a shish pipe.

"I met a man once when I was Admiral Guthrie's aide who had been responsible for checking on hangars at disused airfields at the end of the Second World War. He had been a junior Civil Servant in those days, more than a little wet behind the ears. He used to drive out every other month to check on the equipment in his care. One day he discovered a foundation where a large hangar had once stood.

"He rushed back to his office and told his superior who demanded to see the inventory. Uncapping his gold fountain pen he added one word and handed it back. The item now read 'coat hanger' and my friend had one shilling deducted from his next pay cheque for losing government property!

"But in the case of the Ettrick Bay, you are right. The board found that everything had been done according to the book so we were all exonerated and praised – as First Lieutenant I was gunnery officer so I even got commended for the initiative shown by the gun crew!

"The doctor who treated the yeoman saved his life but could do nothing to save his arm. He praised my coolness under fire. When I asked him later how he had missed my collapse into a pool of my own vomit, he said that the great thing was that I got to my feet and went on with my duties – most people, he said, take days or even weeks to get over something like that. In those days we had barely heard of post-traumatic stress so we didn't suffer much from it.

"The big surprise was sprung by the gunnery Captain. He never said a word about the excessive use of ammunition as I had feared but he praised our record keeping. Then he went on to say that intelligence had reported that an Argentinian jet had made an emergency landing that day with shell damage. Our guys were the only ones who had fired at an aircraft that day so we were credited with a hit.

"The President of the Board of Enquiry almost purred when he heard this: naval gunners being praised by the Royal Artillery may not be unprecedented but it is not an everyday occurrence, I can tell you! Not only were we competent, having avoided any breach of regulations, we were also heroes. You cannot ignore the need for heroes in a war. The public at home want to empathise with the men on the front line and adulation of heroes is an important focus for their support. Medals are sort of thrown into the scales to balance the bad effects on morale at home and amongst the troops of death and life-changing injury."

We had been sitting companionably for some time, having made up more boxes than was justified even by my optimism, while Uncle James told the story. He was engrossed in the ritual of filling and lighting his pipe when I asked:

"So, did you have to give speeches and things?"

"They wanted me to do all that: in fact, they put quite a bit of pressure on me. But it turns out that about the only thing they can't order you to do under Queen's Regulations is to stand up and brag about your supposed heroism!

"When we used up all our supplies I just sailed the 'Ettrick Bay' home and came back up here on demobilisation leave. The Navy was quite keen to let me go since I wouldn't do public appearances.

"The boys on the lifeboats are the real heroes, you know. They go out in the worst weather and do what they can to save people who are unlucky or fools, worthy or unworthy. Everyone a volunteer and they don't look for praise or even thanks.

"So the lads really took the piss at first about my medals but they bought me a few drams while they roasted me and everyone soon agreed to let the whole matter drop – except your Gran!"

Chapter Eleven: *The Wee Escape*

Crime does exist on the island but a close knit community and relative poverty make it less common than in towns and cities. If you lose a rowlock you just open the unlocked door of your neighbours shed and rummage until you find one. Technically it may be burglary but he would have given it to you if he had been there when you needed it.

Other activities considered crimes in the lowlands are not crimes at all in the Highlands. It is the birth right of an islander to take a bird from the air, a fish from the sea and a stag from the hill. The concept of ownership giving one man the right to deny food to another is alien to the Highlander: some of them were jailed for asserting these rights in the late nineteenth century. They came to blows with their landlords when the sheriff sent in a posse of Glasgow Police to Skye to capture the ring-leaders. The women of the Braes, near Portree, routed the forces of law and order, sending them homewards to think again, as the song says!

Smuggling only took hold on the island during the Napoleonic war when the Continental Blockade stopped the import of anil dye from France. Some clever chemist found that the blue dye could be extracted from seaweed so an industry quickly grew on the beaches of the Scottish Islands.

Crofters and their families were employed to stand waist deep in cold water cutting kelp that was hauled up to pits where it was burned and the ash shipped south for processing. In return, cash flooded into the islands but very little of it escaped the pockets of the lairds. The MacDonald's of Sleat on Skye funded the Grand Tour on seaweed and brought back trees from around the World that still adorn their estate. They also built a staircase at a cost of five hundred pounds – more than a million now! In stark contrast, the crofter families continued to live on the very edge of starvation with the added burden of working the kelp beds in the freezing cold sea.

During that period a little smuggling was profitable because there were people with the money to buy the contraband goods, chiefly tobacco from America that took the scenic route from Virginia to Glasgow. A little claret always found its way from France to the West coast of Scotland even when Napoleon was rampaging across Europe establishing the new order that is just gelling after two world wars.

In the modern era there has only ever been one policeman at a time on the island and he has little work to do except when there is an outbreak of foot and mouth or another notifiable disease of livestock. Otherwise the highlight of his year was dressing up to stand upholding the sanctity of elections, local and national, talking to the children in the Primary School and acting as secretary of the Highland Games Committee.

The present bobby was coming under some pressure to pursue convictions but he pointed out, with the backing of the Laird, that his clear-up rate was one hundred per cent; he could hardly be blamed if that was one conviction for one crime. His bosses suspected that the locals had methods other than the courts for dealing with offences but they had no way of proving it.

This policy of local justice saved the lives of two children. Some years ago there was a serial criminal named Patrick but he stole more out of boredom than a desire for worldly possessions. When mains water was introduced, Hamish Toilet ordered a large number of copper boilers and he employed the island's very own Public Enemy Number One to unload them into a barn secured by a padlock that could have been opened by a Boy Scout with a kirby grip.

Next morning the boilers had gone missing from the lock-fast premises but only as far as the criminal mastermind's backyard. The Police

Constable who solved this crime of the century between his morning porridge and his lunchtime dram, was Lachlan. He had been on the island for more than twenty years from the time he entered the police house with his wife and two young children.

Patrick, after a spell in jail, redeemed himself by swimming out to rescue two boys when their dinghy was caught in a sudden squall. He pushed the boat close enough to the shore for others to rescue the youngsters but he drowned before anyone could reach him.

Now Lachlan's wife was dead and his children had moved away, the boy to Glasgow and the girl to Essex. Lachlan moved into a brand new bungalow when he retired and he was happy to potter about his garden during the day, chatting with his cronies in the public bar in the evenings. His son came to visit twice a year and his daughter telephoned him at Christmas. He was a happy man.

Nothing lasts for ever, however, and he began to have the odd brief blackout. The first two, or at least the first two anyone knew about, were in his garden where he was found by the postman lying unconscious. Lachlan convinced him that the cause was dyspepsia and would be cured by a glass of Milk of Magnesia. His third collapse was more public for he folded like a deckchair as he was leaving the bank.

Before he had gathered his wits, he was in hospital undergoing a battery of tests. The doctor put him on medication and reassured him that he had years left in him, but he was adamant that Lachlan could no longer live on his own. Gran went to visit him and received a proposal of marriage. Once he was convinced that wedlock was not the answer to his problem he began to take stock.

His son offered him a room in the bungalow in Bearsden on condition that he stayed out of the kitchen at all times and got rid of his dog.

"I would rather have the dog than that toffee-nosed woman he married. What would I do with myself in Glasgow? They don't even have Gaelic on the road signs."

His son just shrugged when his offer was turned down but the daughter was made of sterner stuff and proved harder to shake off. She took the initiative by finding him a place in a Retirement Home near her four bedroom detached house in Essex: not too near, of course!

"Martin and I don't see nearly enough of you, Father, and your grandsons hardly know you."

"No, Father, BUPA won't let you take a dog! What on earth do you want with that smelly old thing in your lovely new room?"

"I feel like a sheep that's bein' worked by two crafty old dogs that are edging me along a path I do not want to follow," he told Effie and Gran. (After the proposal, Gran decided there was safety in numbers when she was dealing with Lachlan.)

The doctor proved to be wiser in the ways of ageing islanders than any of them. He bided his time until Lachlan was desperate and then offered him a room in the Retirement Home lately opened in the capital of the island. What he would have dismissed contemptuously three weeks before now looked like salvation to the old man and he shook hands on the deal without a moment's hesitation.

"They'll let me have the dog with me during the day but he has to go into a shed at night," he told James and Gran. Then he leant forward and whispered: "To tell you the truth I'm quite pleased because the old beast snores that loud he wakes me up.

"We're not patients or inmates, you know. They call us guests and we have to call them all by their first names – even the matron, although I'm not supposed to call her that.

"They seem to have more rules for us guests than they had in the Polis. Och, they mean well, I suppose."

Uncle James had taken him in a couple of ounces of thick black tobacco.

"They used to sell it by the inch, you know. It would be hanging up in a coil and the storekeeper would just use the cheese knife to cut off two or three inches."

The matron – 'call me Agnes' –was an English woman who had been a frequent visitor with her husband for many years. They had been planning their retirement to the island when he collapsed and died of a heart attack. She brought his ashes to scatter over the moors where they had spent so many happy times hiking and bird watching.

She was in charge of a retirement Home in South Yorkshire and she confided to Effie that she was thinking of changing her bereavement leave into permanent retirement. Effie told her she was too young to think of retiring and that what she needed was a change of scene and a new challenge. She went through to the kitchen to fetch last week's local paper where the job of matron in the island Retirement Home was advertised.

Not one to hang about, Agnes applied for the post that day and was offered the job on a six month trial. This puzzled her because she was by far the best qualified applicant so she went to see the local doctor who had been a non-voting member of the interview panel.

"The problem is that you do not have the Gaelic. A lot of our older folk forget their English when they are very ill or if a bit of dementia sets in. I have no doubt they will confirm you in the post when they see how good you are."

Agnes took the job and applied her modern methods of caring for the elderly with conscientious vigour. She was a bit bossy but kind hearted and she was soon thoroughly settled in to the satisfaction of the whole community. She even started to learn Gaelic.

The only problem was that she had it firmly fixed in her head that speaking in Gaelic was an indicator of nascent senility. If she heard one of her guests speaking the old tongue she would annotate their file '?A' meaning she suspected the onset of Alzheimer's.

"You are allowed to say *feasgar math* or *ciamer a tha thu* but everything else has to be in English," Lachlan complained to James. "I know this is a nice place and she is a kind soul but I do miss my freedom. Do you mind when...." And he and my Uncle would while away an afternoon in reminiscences.

One thing led to another, and before they were finished they had devised a plan to sneak Lachlan out one night to go splash net fishing for sea trout. They may have lacked the charisma of Steve McQueen but they were doughty conspirators.

The Home was locked at night, since some of the guests were inclined to wander, but there was a weak point. The French doors from the day-room were designated a fire exit so the key had to be hung on a hook beside them. The theory was that anyone who would wander off would be too confused to make use of the key. The duty sister carried the rest of the keys with her. They agreed between them that they would make the breakout when Elspeth Campbell was on night duty: "You'll mind her, James. A nice young lassie and a great hand at poaching sea trout." Uncle James thought she would be about fifty–six and he didn't think there was any great skill in poaching a sea trout but he did not want to argue.

On the appointed night, Lachlan waited until all was quiet then crept into the day room and quietly unlocked the French doors. The first problem was that his old dog heard him leave and started whining to be included in the party. When they let him out it took a few minutes to stop him yelping with joy. The second problem arose over what to do with the unlocked doors. In the end they decided to lock them and post the key through the letter box.

"We have to keep the old ones in so the doors have to be locked but the key has to be available in case there's a fire," as Lachlan concluded. "You'll find some way to get me back in, James. I have every confidence!

"You were always a smart lad. I remember that time…" and the pair of them strolled off down to the beach, giving contrasting accounts of the past in happy harmony. I had the dinghy ready with the nets in the stern. Lachlan and James stayed on the shore while I rowed out setting the net around the mouth of a burn. Sea trout have a lot of trouble with lice so they come in to fresh water to get rid of the parasites.

The other two were sharing a large flask of Talisker and still talking, exclusively in Gaelic, of the old days.

"Do you mind the time thon apprentice Minister came out with us? He was enjoying it fine until you went and told him it was illegal to use splash nets. I told him it would be all right because I was the Polis so there was no chance of us being caught, seeing I couldn't be in two places at the same time. He still thought he might end up in Hell for the sin of it!"

By this time I was inside the net splashing the flat of the oar blade on the water to scare the fish out to sea into the net. The other pair threw in a stone or two as their contribution but they were too busy lowering the level of whisky in the flask to take much notice of what was going on in the water. The dog was racing up and down the shingle barking and whimpering in ecstasy.

There were two nice fish in the net when I brought it in and I made all tidy before I joined the discussion on how to return Lachlan to the fold. We drifted towards the Home still without a viable plan. The dog began to get fed up with the inactivity so he started to give little yelps to attract our attention. I thought he would have been tired out but he was even fresher than Lachlan who was clearly determined to delay his return as long as possible.

"Agnes always sleeps with her window open. The lad could climb up and get in quietly and creep downstairs and let me in."

"Is she a heavy sleeper?"

"I have no idea. In fact that seems like an improper suggestion. How would I learn her sleeping habits?"

The effect of the whisky was causing the men to forget that discreet whispers were required, and it wasn't long before Elspeth Campbell came out and told us to be quiet. She didn't seem to be at all surprised to find one of her charges standing swaying on the wrong side of the door.

"Come in to the kitchen the three of you, and for heaven's sake keep your voices down or you'll have the whole house up. Well yes I will have a wee sensation from the flask if only to stop the pair of you getting even more drunk." This last in response to an offer from Lachlan who had taken charge of the water of life.

I went out to fetch the fish which they decided would be the main course on tomorrow's menu. I gutted and cleaned them so it was a few minutes before I got back. By that time all three of them were mellow bordering on the merry. Lachlan was extravagantly praising Elspeth's skill at cooking sea trout, when the door opened and Agnes came in wearing a flannel dressing gown and with some sort of paper bows in her hair.

In the ensuing silence you could have heard an arthritic knee creak.

"Next time you have a little adventure, I would be grateful if you take me along," she announced, and with that she turned on her heel and went out closing the door gently behind her!

Chapter Twelve: *Foreign Travel*

Lachlan and the Minister arrived on the island within a few years of each other and had a great many things in common. Of course, they were both concerned with the well-being of the people, one caring for their spiritual needs while the other protected their lives and property. They were both stern moralists but equally forgiving of human lapses. They very quickly established themselves in the community although both had been brought up in cities.

The parallels went further: each had a city-bred wife with one son and one daughter. The Minister's youngest was in the same class as Lachlan's eldest and the two girls were officially 'best friends'. All the children were bright and went on to university and to lives on the mainland. Having said all that, the similarities were more apparent than real. Lachlan was brought up in a Gaelic speaking home in Inverness while the Minister, Mr Dinwoodie, was from Greenock. Lachlan had met his wife when, as a young constable, he had toured the pawn shops with lists of stolen property. She always claimed that she helped out in an antique shop although she didn't need the money. She always made a point of going to local auction sales and giving an expert opinion on china and paintings.

The minister's wife was the daughter of a Writer to Her Majesty's Signet and she had been educated in private schools until she was despatched to the Domestic Science College in Glasgow by her Father who considered the law too logical and, therefore, too difficult for a mere woman. Her two brothers followed their father into the law and became

WS – one had become an advocate and was now a judge.

By tradition, a hockey match was played each year between the ladies of the Dough School, as the College was known, and the gentlemen of the Divinity College. It tended to be a somewhat one-sided affair since the gentlemen knew very little about the game and the girls were no ladies when it came to sport. The Minister was over six foot tall and he played rugby for the university. He was given the task of opposing a nifty winger, about an inch more than five foot tall and, in those days, very slim.

She was then, as now, a feisty woman who had learned to hold her own against her brothers, so she was undaunted by the size of her opponent. Her whole-hearted enthusiasm with the hockey stick in this fateful match led directly to marriage and children! In the first five minutes she managed to land telling blows on the shins of the lofty divinity student. The last hit was a full-blooded strike to the ankle that resulted in the lad being helped off by his diminutive assailant. Her remorse being on a par with her enthusiasm, she stayed with him until he felt fit to return to the unequal fray.

The match continued in their absence and their teammates only noticed that they had not returned when the whistle blew for half-time and they were discovered with their lips surgically welded together and their bodies entwined. Forty years later despite marriage and two kids, they were still as affectionate with each other although they now limited their public display to pecks on the cheek and holding hands when they walked about the capital.

Lachlan's wife never really settled on the island and she and her children remained rather aloof. The boy was a decent shinty player and was accepted in the community for that ability but the girl was always an outsider. She always stayed on the fringes of activities and would look on with what was widely regarded as a superior smile; the less forgiving even called it a sneer.

Mrs Dinwoodie descended on the island like an equinoctial gale. She made pastoral visits to every home regardless of whether it was occupied by church members, agnostics, Catholics or even new age druids. She is still making the visits and counts white witches and the Roman Catholic priest amongst her special friends. Domestically, she learned to milk a cow and mastered Gaelic in six months. She now taught the language in the Primary School and offered evening classes in conversational Gaelic to incomers.

The two women met for the first time the day Lachlan moved into the police house. Mrs Dinwoodie took the baby boy and the girl, Elspeth, who was about six years old, so their Mother could concentrate on the organisational aspects of the flitting.

When the Minister came home for lunch, his wife left him to change the baby's disgusting nappy and took Elspeth with her to milk the cow. It was customary to milk morning and evening but Mrs Dinwoodie had a theory, in obedience to which she milked only when the family needed it. The little girl watched, wide eyed, as the teats were washed with disinfectant than squeezed and pulled to send the milk foaming into a galvanised pail firmly held between the thighs of the Minister's wife. Elspeth did not say a word when the milk was poured through muslin into a jug and carried in to be placed in the centre of the lunch table, still warm.

It was only when Mr Dinwoodie poured her a glass that she broke her silence.

"No thank you. I get my milk from a bottle not a dirty old cow."

After school she took herself off to university in London losing her Highland accent overnight. Her brother took a degree in engineering at Glasgow Caledonian University and, after a few years in the Arabian Gulf, married and settled in Bearsden. The Minister's children went to Edinburgh University where they lived with their grandparents. The boy followed his father into the church while the girl, Heather, returned to an older family tradition and is now a WS. Her Grandfather was as proud as punch when she came top in her University class and vehemently denied that he ever thought women were unqualified for the legal profession.

"Did he think I really yearned to be a pastry cook?" Mrs Dinwoodie asked in outrage when she was told that he had recanted.

As a child, Heather had all of her Mother's spirit but topping five foot eight inches before her fifteenth birthday was an inheritance straight from her Father. She preferred fishing and football to dolls and dresses, unlike Elspeth who considered that anything you had to do out of doors was 'rough' and unladylike. Because of the coincidence of their ages and the positions of their Fathers in the community, they were expected to be friends. Heather was, indeed, the only friend Elspeth had when they were growing up but the pair of them had so little in common that it must have been painful to see them together.

Before she graduated, Elspeth met an older man in a wine bar who was 'something in the city'. He wooed her, won her and carried her off to a detached house in Essex with a garden not a lot bigger than Hampden Park. She happily abandoned her degree and set about providing her financier husband with two sons and lavish, well-planned dinners for his business contacts. Lachlan said it was more a merger than a marriage with joint assets taking the place of love.

They travelled a lot in pursuit of his business, leaving the boys with their nanny. However, they also had two family holidays in the year. During the Easter school holidays, they would fly to Spain to their villa; Elspeth always stayed an extra week to liaise with the local agent who looked after and leased the property during the summer. Since her clothing allowance came out of the rental fees she had a personal interest in ensuring everything went smoothly.

The second holiday always involved driving to a destination in Continental Europe. Rome one year, Vienna another and so on, always staying at good hotels and dining in the best restaurants.

The year that Lachlan went into a Home, her father-in-law died before Easter and, while she did not let that interfere with the family time in Spain, Elspeth felt obliged to invite the new widow to join them on their planned holiday to the French Pyrenees and Andorra. Although the boys were growing up there would be ample space in the back seat of the BMW since mother-in-law was slightly built. The problem of the extra baggage was solved by fitting a roof rack.

The journey started well with Elspeth quelling an incipient rebellion.

"She smells, Mother."

"I am quite sure she doesn't - she is your Grandmother, after all. Just be nice to her if you still want to go to Spa next month for the grand prix."

The old lady was a little careless in her eating habits, so Elspeth insisted on her having her meals early with the boys in the hotel dining room.

"It will be far too tiring for you, Mother, to get all dressed up to dine with us." She could then put on a glamorous frock and dine in the most expensive place in town with a feeling of complacent righteousness.

Sight-seeing, which provided the photo opportunities so essential for showing friends what a wonderful time they always had, was a little slower than usual but Granny was willing to make the effort to keep up, encouraged by Elspeth's exhortations. At the start of the second week, they were a little late arriving in Carcassonne and had to rather rush the gruelling tour of the walls They had a four star hotel booked in Perpignan and there was a restaurant that had been personally recommended by a Deputy Governor of the Bank of England when Elspeth met him at a city dinner, so they could not afford to dawdle.

Granny was a bit red-faced and rather breathless by the time they got back to the car but she took her accustomed place in the back seat between the boys without complaint. About ten minutes after they set off she gave a little groan and slumped against the elder boy. He tried to shove her off without alerting his Mother but a harder push than he intended resulted in Granny falling forward against the front seats.

They pulled into the first lay-by and satisfied themselves that the old lady had died. Her son wanted to try artificial respiration or calling an ambulance but he accepted his wife's assurance that nothing could be done to revive the deceased and that the best course of action was to get back in the car and drive to a police station in Perpignan.

While their parents had been discussing their plans, the boys had hauled Granny out of the back seat and laid her on the grass. The younger one had even crossed her hands over her chest as he had seen them do in the movies.

For the first time in her life, Elspeth faced open revolt: her sons flatly refused to sit in the back of the car with a corpse. She tried all her armoury of bribes, threats and, finally, tears but to no avail. She even stooped so low as to demand of her husband that he do something about it. It was the elder boy who proposed the solution that she was forced to accept.

They took the suitcases from the roof rack and put Granny up in their place. The boys could hardly complain about sharing the back seat with luggage, especially when they saw the look on their Mother's face.

They drove the twenty odd miles to Perpignan at a modest speed out of respect for the body on the roof and stopped outside the first gendarmerie that they came to. They parked outside and the parents got out of the car; the boys joined them on the pavement and another argument developed.

"There might be bodily fluids," said the younger boy who was going through that stage when he read nothing but Point horror.

Elspeth had just about had enough by this stage. She recognised that if she was to reassert her authority she would have to make some concessions. She turned, without another word, and stormed into the police station followed by her husband and sons. The stress caused her to forget much of her French which was fluent, colloquial and delivered in an impeccable accent, so it was left to her husband to exercise his schoolboy French rusty from long disuse.

It took about ten minutes to explain the situation to a patient gendarme who had learned enough English to be confused. Then they all trooped out led by the gendarme to find that the BMW was no longer where they had left it. The car, complete with deceased Granny had been stolen and it was never recovered!

Chapter Thirteen: *The Gift Horse*

I spent the whole summer on the island the year I went to university, from the end of my Highers to the start of Fresher's Week in late September. I was very willing to work on the croft but after the hay was cut on the few acres under grass there was very little to do until the potatoes were ready for lifting. Uncle James enjoyed doing the little that was necessary, telling me to enjoy this period of freedom before the serious business started in October at Gilmorehill.

I was frequently, I have to admit, in a quandary about how to fill my hours. I still tramped the moors and wandered along the beach but I had grown out of the ability to find adventure in these diversions. I no longer expected to meet Alan Breck Stewart or the Master of Ballantrae around the next bend or lying wounded in the lea of every peat stack.

Much of my time was spent out in the dinghy fishing but it was difficult to find anyone with time to spare to accompany me. Until, that is, I asked Lachlan, the retired policeman if he fancied landing a few rock cod. From that day on he was constantly ready, smiling in anticipation and miserably disappointed when I had something else to do.

I would arrange to meet him and by the time I had rowed round and put the nose of the dinghy on the shingle he would be wading in to make us fast, dressed in wellie boots and a North Face jacket. He was often accompanied by the matron of the retirement home he lived in.

"Call me Agnes: I feel so old when you call me 'matron; or 'Mrs.'"

"Call me Lachlan, for I'm younger at heart than she ever was!"

He handed her into the boat like a courtier and baited the hooks for her since she was squeamish about handling the lugworm we used as bait. This was a woman who had assisted at operations and had laid out corpses but there is nowt, as she herself often said, as queer as folk! She fussed over him making sure his scarf was in place and bringing a towel to put on the seat so he would not get a wet bum. They were so like my idea of an old married couple as to be almost a caricature!

Agnes was learning Gaelic and was keen to try it out on the fishing trips. I had achieved a vocabulary of almost fifty words in all the years I had been visiting Uncle James and Aunt Effie so she treated me as a hopeless case. She kept trying to induce Lachlan to help her learn the old tongue but he was mockingly dismissive of her efforts.

The problem went back to the time of her arrival as matron when she got the idea that the locals only spoke Gaelic when they were losing touch with reality. She had marked Lachlan down as '?A' (her code for 'possible onset of Alzheimer's') on his record and it still rankled with him.

They sat side-by-side in the stern with their shoulders touching while I rowed from the bow with the bucket of bait and the catch flapping about on the floorboards between us. Lachlan always handed Agnes into the dinghy but if they were not on friendly terms he would sit on her left. Since he was almost totally deaf in his right ear this meant that he could not converse with her. When they were getting on well he sat on her right and they chatted the whole time we were out. I say 'chatted' but it sounded more like bickering to the casual listener!

"Sit still woman! The fish will be thinking you have the St Vitus dance!"

"Well, at least I can sit here for an hour without having to go to the loo!"

This gibe had me holding my breath while I waited for Lachlan to respond. I was relieved when he laughed and gently punched her shoulder. On our last trip he had started squirming and he got very red in the face. Finally he growled at me to pass the baler, a galvanised pot with a handle: a bit like a mini-wok. Agnes turned disdainfully away while he struggled with his zip and waited, giving little tugs until the flow started. She sang a Gaelic song that the island choir were rehearsing for a ceilidh but nothing could have drowned out the sound of piddle hitting galvanised iron.

I enjoyed listening to them talking about past times that were still real to them, although they were history to me. I mean, they were about when the Beatles started; Lachlan had been to hear Billy Connolly before he was taken up by the English!

They treated each other in much the same way as the boys and girls at school did – insults and shoves were a clear sign that you fancied someone and were fancied in return. Not surprisingly, I presumed that Lachlan and Agnes had something going on although I drew the line at imagining them snogging (gross!!)which was the next development for my school mates.

Uncle James said there was nothing going on between them but I am still very confused: if you follow the same path you must surely arrive at the same destination.

Most of Lachlan's stories were about policing and almost all the tales were about his time on the island as its only representative of law and order. I knew that he had moved there from his home town of Inverness and I just assumed that he had joined the police force in his native city. The Scottish parliament had been discussing the reorganisation of policing in Scotland and I asked Lachlan what he thought about it.

"Och, they're never content to leave well alone. When I joined they still had amateur Chief Constables."

It turned out that he had joined a county constabulary in the Scottish central belt. He had applied to join the Northern Constabulary but they had not offered him a post although they did say they would put him on their waiting list.

"I was only allowed to transfer to the Highland force to keep me quiet: I knew too much, you see."

"You knew where the bodies were buried?" I was still going

through a phase.

"Not exactly bodies, but certainly where actual bodily harm had been hushed up."

Following a tradition going back to the foundation of the force, the Chief Constable was appointed when he retired as colonel of a Guards regiment. He was related to half the nobs in the county and more than half the policemen had served in his old regiment, mostly long after he retired. His old batman had retired at the same time as The Colonel, as everyone called him, and was still serving in the rank of constable.

The two men had served together throughout the Second World War, mostly in the North African desert and The Colonel still had a very soft spot for his old comrade in arms. The trouble was that the batman liked a dram. It was all right at first, but after his wife died his toping got out of control. The Colonel spent some effort on devising ingenious ways to keep the batman out of trouble and had succeeded at least in keeping him out of the dock. He had sold the family home and now lived in squalor in a police apartment intended for new recruits. Since he was struggling to fund his habit even on full pay, The Colonel had extended his service and he had completed thirty-four years on the force. His meagre pension and the rocketing price of whisky would have left him destitute.

As Chief Constable, The Colonel was able to shield the old man but he could not keep his condition a secret from all the police officers and nearly all of the solicitors in the county. The community was prepared to tolerate the deception because The Colonel was well liked and universally respected. They survived in the shadow of Glasgow and it was felt that any breath of scandal leaking out would give their big city neighbours an excuse to move in.

The support of the Chief Constable for his batman was considered rather eccentric but the popular view was that the old man had probably saved The Colonel's life or honour when they served together.

Shortly after Lachlan joined the force, the outside world intruded on this cosy, if ragged, arrangement. Her Majesty's Inspector of

Constabulary notified the Chief Constable that an inspection team would be visiting the county to make a critical review of the force. This was no more than routine so The Colonel passed the papers to a deputy and told him to apply a bit of spit and polish.

"What you can't bring up to standard, hide!" was his only contribution. It was very well understood that the first thing to be hidden was the batman. He would not take leave except when The Colonel was on holiday so they could not simply send him down to Saltcoats for a few days while the inspection team was ferreting around.

The standard procedure was for The Colonel to get him drunk then lock him in his flat until the danger was past but this time the head of the visiting team announced his intention of inspecting the living accommodation for single officers and the houses occupied by married policemen. The Chief Constable felt stymied.

As luck would have it The Colonel's love of golf, that began when the stymie was part of the rules, gave him a slim chance to avoid disaster. His regular golf partner was the head of a local firm of solicitors, called George McBeth. This man was a church elder and of such rectitude that he would only prosecute in criminal cases, leaving defence briefs to his junior partners. He spent a month every summer as a lay preacher at missions held in English seaside resorts. It almost goes without saying that he was a county councillor and had twice been provost of his home town.

He was married to a quiet, self-effacing woman and had two children, a boy and a girl, at the local secondary school. On the Saturday, a week before the inspectors were to arrive, George and The Colonel won the Bruce cup, the premier trophy for golf in the county. The victory was particularly sweet since they thrashed their great rivals, another solicitor and a professor of surgery in a Glasgow teaching hospital.

In the early hours of the Sunday morning, the Chief Constable was awakened by a telephone call from this surgeon calling from the Cottage Hospital. The professor refused to give any details on the telephone, a wise precaution in those days before automatic exchanges were in common use.

Most of the job satisfaction for a telephone operator came from listening in to calls and a call from the hospital to the police chief would have been irresistible!

When he arrived, The Colonel was ushered into the recovery room adjoining the operating theatre where Mrs McBeth was lying, still unconscious from the operation that had set her broken shoulder and wired her jaw, broken in two places. Councillor MacBeth proudly acknowledged that he was a martinet and there had been rumours that his iron fist was sometimes applied with too much vigour to his family members.

The Colonel spoke to the son, a lad of about fifteen who was sitting in the matron's office, with anger and fear chasing each other across his ashen face.

"He's always knocking her about," the lad confided. "It's bad enough when he's sober but he came home well plastered with that golf trophy thing; and he had more when he got in. My sister was out at the flicks with her pals and she got back about fifteen minutes late.

"She was all happy when she came in. Excited, you know, and wanting to tell our Mum about the movie and everything. He just totally lost his temper with her and when Mum tried to stop him he went nuts! He hit her with the poker! I thought he had killed her – he thought so, too, because he dropped the fire iron and knelt beside her crying and praying.

"I called the Hospital and the professor came with the ambulance driver. Will they put him away? I would jail him and throw away the key!"

"Where is your father now?"

"He phoned the minister even before the ambulance got there. The pair of them will be on their knees in the manse, expecting God to forgive him."

The Colonel left the boy with the matron and went to find Mr McBeth. He was beginning to sober up with the help of black coffee forced on him by the minister's wife. The Colonel himself was feeling a bit guilty because he had encouraged George to have a few more drinks than were good for the pair of them before they left the golf club, scene of their triumph. It did not take long, however, for his remorse to turn to an icy rage when the solicitor started wallowing in maudlin self-pity.

"She was asking for it," he slurred. "How can I hope to bring my children up to praise the Lord and honour their parents if I do not chastise them when they err? She tried to stop me doing my fatherly – my Christian – duty so she has to bear the consequences of her sin."

The Colonel told him that there was no possible excuse for the level of violence McBeth had used.

"Your poor wife will be in hospital for several weeks and the prof. says that she may have restricted use of her right shoulder for the rest of her life."

"You're wrong! She cannot remain in hospital. Who will cook and keep house for me and my poor bairns if she idles in a hospital bed?"

Before the day-shift started, Mrs McBeth was transferred to a private ward in the professor's teaching hospital. The two nurses and an orderly who constituted the night staff were warned of the dire consequences if they breathed a word about the events of the night as they went off duty.

At one o'clock on the Monday afternoon, the Chief Constable convened a meeting in the professor's office that was also attended by the procurator fiscal and a leading solicitor. They first visited Mrs McBeth who was conscious but heavily sedated. It was quickly agreed that the matter was serious and that something had to be done but only the medical man considered that criminal proceedings were appropriate.

"Think of the damage it would do to the legal profession in the county if we put George in the dock," the fiscal said.

"It was attempted murder, man. You can't let him get off scot free!"

"Actual bodily harm, perhaps, but not, surely, attempted murder? A man has a right to discipline his family although there is no disagreement amongst us that George went a wee bit farther than the situation merited."

At this point a sober and somewhat subdued George was invited to join them. He said he was sorry but wanted to make it clear that the blame rested with the excess of alcohol he had consumed rather than any fundamental flaw in his character.

"Everything would have been fine if that daft lad of mine hadn't panicked and called the hospital," he concluded.

As a plea for mitigation it failed dismally but it did give the professor an idea. He suggested that the councillor should accept voluntary commitment to a closed asylum for treatment of alcoholism. There was general approval of the idea and Mr McBeth accepted after his suggestion that they just forget it had happened was scornfully rejected.

The Procurator Fiscal agreed to drop criminal proceedings in return for the lawyer getting treatment but he made two stipulations. The first was that a voluntary commitment was not acceptable and that George should be sectioned under the Mental Health Act; the second proviso was that Mrs McBeth should agree to drop charges against her husband.

The professor and the doctor in charge of the poor woman signed the committal papers there and then. The colonel and the fiscal went in to the ward to explain things to the patient and get her consent to their plan.

"She couldn't write because of her broken shoulder and she couldn't speak because her jaw is wired shut but we are satisfied that she understood and agreed to our proposals," they reported to the ad hoc committee when they left the ward.

Mrs McBeth's sister moved into the house to look after the kids while McBeth moved in with The Colonel under informal house arrest. A rumour was spread that Mrs McBeth had suffered a nervous breakdown and that the couple had left on an extended world cruise: no date was given for their return.

It was Wednesday before the Colonel came up with a clever plan to solve all his problems at the same time. Only one thing remained to be fixed and the lot fell to Lachlan. He was young, had a driving licence and was known not to have made many friends since he joined the force.

The plan started at seven-thirty am on the following Monday when an unmarked police car, driven by Lachlan and carrying The Colonel's batman and councillor McBeth set off for Lochgilphead. The team from the Inspectorate of Constabulary was not due to arrive until nine o'clock, by which time a team of women police constables had been sent to thoroughly clean the batman's flat.

The Colonel came down himself to see them on their way to Argyll. He took Lachlan aside and told him to drive carefully making sure that he did not get back before five pm on the next day. He then frisked the two older men, removing a flask of whisky from each of them. He loaded a hamper with food and soft drinks before he had a final word with Lachlan.

"You have fuel for the whole journey. If they need a pee, stop in a lay-by not less than five miles from licensed premises."

Everything went according to plan. The Colonel took the inspection team around the police apartments on Monday afternoon and was commended on the quality and neatness of the accommodation. He explained that the two empty flats were occupied by officers on detached duty.

George and the batman discovered that they had both been in Italy at the end of the War so they swapped stories of wine, women and war for the whole journey. Lachlan enjoyed driving, the scenery reminded him of home and he was amused by the tall stories coming from the back seat as the two old warriors tried to prove that the unit they had served with was the best in the army.

Arrived at the asylum, the three of them sat in a waiting room for a few minutes, then a muscular male nurse carrying a clipboard came in and looked at them sitting side by side. They made an interesting contrast. Lachlan was young, glowing with health and wearing a sports jacket that was rather tight across the shoulders since his mum had bought it for him when he was seventeen before he filled out. The batman was wearing his shabby demob suit and the five hours he had endured since his last drink of spirits were beginning to show: his face was blotchy and clammy with sweat. Mr McBeth was by far the best dressed of the three, sitting calm and relaxed in a well-tailored business suit.

Without hesitation the nurse went up to the batman who was sitting in the middle.

"Will you come with me, please, sir? There is some paperwork that has to be completed."

The batman got up with a bit of a shove from Lachlan, wiped his sweating palms on his trousers and followed the nurse through a second door at the back of the waiting room.

"I thought nothing of it," Lachlan told me. "He was the senior officer so it was right that he should be picked out although I did wonder if he could hold a pen, his hands were shaking that much. I was left alone with Mr McBeth and we had nothing much to say to each other. I tried him with football – surely every Scotsman can talk about football – but he didn't even know how the local team was doing, though it turned out he was one of the directors!"

They sat there in an increasingly uneasy silence for about thirty minutes before someone came in, saw them, and hurried out again Next minute a doctor came in and asked what they were waiting for. Lachlan explained that they were waiting for his fellow officer who had been called away to sign something or other.

"So who are you?" the doctor asked, turning to George.

"I am councillor McBeth, your new patient," George replied rising from his seat and offering his hand to the doctor with a broad smile. "Pleased to meet you."

So the batman was released after they had got him dressed again in his shiny demob suit and they headed back to civilisation. He admitted that he had been a wee bit confused but thought that getting into pyjamas was maybe a routine that all visitors had to endure.

The senior doctor was fairly apologetic for picking the wrong man as his patient, but he was at pains to point out that he was satisfied that they had picked the person most in need of treatment for alcoholism!

We were booked into a hotel near Arrochar for the night where the proprietor turned out to be The Colonel's former adjutant. He and the batman made serious inroads into the whisky reserves while Lachlan flirted with the barmaid while he made a half pint last the whole evening.

Back at base he received a commendation from The Colonel himself. It was not until he reported for duty the next day that he discovered the sting in the tail. After the briefing for the Two-to-Ten shift, the sergeant asked him to wait behind for a moment.

"You know you will have to go."

When Lachlan protested that The Colonel had personally praised him, the sergeant shook his head.

"They have to get rid of you. You know too many secrets. You know you will keep your mouth shut and I trust you but there are people involved who think everyone is as twisted and self-seeking as themselves."

Sure enough, two weeks later Lachlan was told that he was being transferred to the Northern Constabulary who, according to the Chief Inspector who gave him the news, had specially requested him by name!

"How many are on the waiting list to join this force?" Lachlan asked the Inspector who welcomed him in Inverness.

"We don't have a waiting list. We sign them up quick in case they change their minds!"

Chapter Fourteen: *Having Your Cake and Eating It*

I applied for a provisional driver's licence before my seventeenth birthday so I could start my motoring career as soon as the clock struck midnight. I had accepted, reluctantly, that I was not going to play football for Scotland but from Jim Clark and Jackie Stewart to David Coulthard and Paul di Resta I had shining examples to follow onto the Formula One tracks of the world. My Dad insisted that I take proper lessons and my Gran gave me twenty-four lessons (for the price of twenty, which pleased her) as my main birthday present.

Of course, I wanted to be behind the wheel day and night with brief halts to eat and pee but Dad would not let me drive his car with him as the qualified driver.

"You might pick up all my bad habits."

"But you're the police! How can you have bad driving habits?"

"I'm a detective who drives a four year old Ford Mondeo. You must be thinking of the flash lads on the motorway patrol driving souped-up BMWs. We have a gentleman's agreement: they don't tell me how to solve murders and I don't do handbrake turns!"

He was adamant so I had to wait, making no effort to conceal my impatience, for my weekly lessons in the dual-control Astra favoured by my instructor. He was ex Royal Air Force and had taught generations of recruits how to handle anything from staff cars through fire engines and up to the Queen Mary transporters that could carry a whole aeroplane.

Dealing with impatient, incompetent seventeen-year-olds was probably just as hazardous!

I passed my test, first time, just after Easter and started adding hours to my driving experience. Now that he could not ruin my driving style with his bad habits, Dad was happy for me to take the wheel for family outings. He even let me out on my own to visit a friend who had moved to Largs! Of course, I had to phone when I arrived and phone again just before I started home but that did not spoil the treat of being alone. In sole control of a motor vehicle – even a four year old Mondeo!

When I went to the island after my Highers I had fretfully few opportunities to indulge my passion. James had an old van and an even older tractor but there are not that many places to go and only three decent roads to go on. I assiduously offered to take Aunt Effie shopping or to pick up groceries for her – preferably one item at a time so I could drive another twelve miles – the round trip distance from the croft to the capital.

I was wondering if I should go home so that my driving skills would not atrophy when the Laird asked me to drive him in his Volvo to Glasgow airport. I jumped at the chance! Since he had intervened to convince Dad that I should go to University, the Laird and I had become really good friends. I had gone to the big house to pay my respects and I probably mentioned in passing that I had a driver's licence. In truth, I may have mentioned that fact more than once in the course of the half hour we spent together!

He did not pay a great deal of attention to what I was saying because he was wrestling with a problem. Some years before, his estate had given several acres of ground close to the beach to the council. They had laid a tarmacadam runway and put up a two-storey corrugated iron shed to double as control tower and terminal for the island airfield. The runway was short but could handle helicopters and light, piston and turboprop 'planes. This was enough to provide emergency services to link us with Inverness and Glasgow.

Outgoing patients were often expectant mothers who had

developed late complications: more than one baby had first seen the light of day at a thousand feet approaching Raigmore Hospital. The Cottage Hospital took in a fairly steady stream of minor injuries to climbers who were almost as prolific as midges in the summer months. The island did not have anything more majestic or challenging itself than a few Grahams but it was roughly at the centre of a circle of Monroes. The rescue helicopter was an all too frequent visitor.

A few tourists arrived on the twelve-seater aeroplane that was the biggest that could land. Three flights a week to Glasgow were scheduled and there were probably five or six charter flights in the season. The aircraft were propeller driven and made so little noise that they hardly disturbed the colony of terns that nested in the rocky foreshore just below the airstrip.

Now the council was threatening the Laird with the compulsory purchase of more land so the airstrip could be extended to accommodate jet liners. The European Union was offering big grants to councils to improve tourism in remote areas. The island had the status of a parish with only two representatives on the main council. The Laird was opposed to the development and was supported in his opposition by the great majority of the islanders. He had the backing of the parish council but one of the proper councillors was a White Settler who owned a hotel.

The Laird thought that reasoned argument about the unsuitability of a large airstrip on a small island would prevail but, with the active support of the hotelier/councillor, his reservations were ignored and he was to be forced to provide the land for the extension. By the time I spoke to him, he had realised that he would need sound legal advice quickly if he was to stop what he saw as a disastrous mistake.

He had maintained good contacts from his days as a barrister and he knew just the person he wanted to brief. The woman was now a silk, head of chambers and there were persistent rumours that she was on the verge of being appointed to the bench. The Laird thought that she was less likely to drop everything and argue his case against the council if he wrote to her so he decided to see her in person. I think they may have had a bit of a history, because he was pretty confident that she would not refuse him face-to-face.

He drove his old Land Rover to the airstrip two days after I talked to him to take the scheduled flight to Glasgow and an onward connection to London. The only other passenger that day was the councillor who supported the extension. While they waited for the incoming flight to land he could not resist a sneer when the Laird told him he was on his way to take his protest to law.

"You can't even protest against progress without using our airstrip."

The Laird did not say a word. He just got into his Land Rover, letting the flight leave without him, and came to the croft to talk to Uncle James. I had never seen the Laird really angry before.

"I will not give up! I suppose I'll just have to drive to Glasgow but you know how I hate driving off the island."

"I'll drive! I mean, I would be very happy to drive you to Glasgow, if it would help."

Both men had probably forgotten that I was there for they turned as one and stared at me. I had had a licence for two months, as they both knew, so the only real surprise was that they considered the idea at all! Consider it they did, for the most part talking about me as if I was not there. I did not disclose that my longest single journey at that time was about twenty miles!

Eventually the Laird said that it was very good of me but since I had just arrived from Glasgow it would not be fair to expect me to go straight back. I soon made it clear that I would drive to the gates of the Bar-L and sign in for a fortnight just so long as I could drive.

Looking back, I can see that he was seeking a way to let me down gently; he knew I lacked the skill and experience but he was too kind, too aware of the fragile confidence of an seventeen year old boy, to refuse. He could probably foresee driving most of the way himself.

I set off on a tour of the island to get the feel of the Laird's Volvo that was much bigger and heavier than anything I had been in before. Then I picked him up and drove to the ferry. I negotiated the ramp with my heart racing and my breath stopped but I was able to park anywhere on the deck because the traffic was so light. Driving off the ferry was a dawdle and I began to really enjoy myself. The Laird did not speak on the journey except to give directions

"I'll just let you concentrate. You have enough to do without me chattering in your ear."

He had said that he would take over to give me a break but when we left the Croit Anna in Fort William after lunch he refused the car keys when I passed them to him.

"You drive, young fellow. In fact, do you know? I wouldn't mind you driving all the way to London if you felt up to it."

This is what heaven feels like! He may have offered me the present trip out of kindness but he had just given me a ringing endorsement: I savoured it.

I spent the night at home after dropping the Laird at a hotel. My room is at the front of the house and I left my curtains open all night so I could look out at the Volvo – my Volvo – solid and gleaming in the moonlight

The next day we let the rush hour snarl by and then took the motorway south to Gretna and England. The Laird had arranged for us to stay with an old friend of his father's so we were heading for the Cheshire countryside.

"Will he have room for both us?"

The Laird laughed until he choked. "He could accommodate a coachload!"

We travelled in companionable silence. I was feeling very comfortable in the big Volvo. The only problem was in keeping the speed down to somewhere not too far above the legal limit. He directed me in an unflurried way giving me plenty time to get into the proper lane and advised me on the width and twistiness of the roads we used after we left the motorway. After several miles on an 'A' class road we turned into leafy lanes until finally he directed me through old brick gate posts onto an unmarked minor road.

The road surface was good and it gently curved through an avenue of mature chestnut and beech trees. After perhaps half a mile the trees ended to show that we were on a drive bending around to finish in front of a mansion. Standing at the stairs outside the huge front door was an old man angrily waving a stick at us.

"Why are you stopping?" the Laird asked. I pointed at the man who had now added a capering dance to his stick waving.

"The Baron must have become impatient and decided to come out to meet us."

The waving stick, it appeared, was a friendly greeting and the red face was a legacy of years of drinking vintage port. I drove on to the bottom of the stairs leading to the door to be met by the old man still capering about but now grinning at the Laird.

"We're in the West Wing now," he began while we were still trudging up to his level. "It's not the best maintained bit but I leave the rest of the pile for the tourists who still flock, if a little less densely, to see how the other half scrape by."

When the Laird commented on his stick, the baron thumped it on the ground and sighed. "I'm just getting old, my boy. I would rather have this dodgy knee than be like my poor Mary; she has no physical impairment at all but the poor love's wits have fled – she doesn't know whether it's Tuesday or Euston Station."

We were shown to our rooms in the poorly maintained West Wing. I had rather expected a tin bath and a potty under the bed but my room was sumptuous with a modern bathroom suite, plasma television and even an internet jack!

"Don't dress for dinner" turned out to be a reference to the style of clothing rather than an invitation to communal nudity. At my Dad's suggestion I had brought a jacket but I had no tie. The Laird appeared in his kilt and hairy tweed hunting jacket while our host was resplendent in Norfolk jacket and plus-fours.

I said very little at dinner being still in a state of shock. I had never conceived of anything like this place – it was comparable in size to Buckingham Palace! We were served by an old couple, he in dark trousers with a striped waistcoat, while she had on a frilly snow-white apron over a black dress – she even had on a white frilly bonnet. It would have looked quite sexy on someone forty years younger.

The meal was served in the little dining room, somewhat smaller than a ballroom and with a table that could only have sat about sixteen people in comfort. The main dining room *was* the size of a ballroom and had been used as such. That table was of the extending variety and when all the extra pieces were in place it could seat eighty!

After dinner the Baron left us to see to what he called 'the changing of the guard'. His wife, lost to dementia, needed constant attention and he made a point of thanking the day nurse and welcoming the night nurse.

The Laird and I went to a library that had more books than the Mitchell Library, or so it seemed to me looking up at the ranks stretching from the floor into the dimness beyond reach of the fire and table lamps that focused on three comfortable armchairs. I had never seen the Laird smoke but he accepted a huge cigar from a silver humidor. He cut it with a gold cutter and got it drawing with casual competence.

"Tell the lad how you came to own this heap," he said when the Baron re-joined us, looking gloomy, and both Havanas were drawing well so that the air become misty with an aromatic blue haze.

The old man chuckled. "This stripling," he nodded towards the Laird, "is my godson. His Father and I were at school together – I still miss the Colonel, you know. The boy never did have any respect for age and business acumen."

"Business acumen my left foot. A conman and a chancer was all you ever were!" the Laird riposted.

The Baron's chuckle became a cough and he put the cigar down with obvious regret telling us that his doctor had told him to give them up.

"My father was a weaver – not one of your Highland weavers with one loom in a corner of the living room and debts above his ankles. My father, like his father and grandfather before him, was a factory owner who wove cloth by the furlong. During the Second World War he was one of several mill owners contracted to supply cloth first for the armed forces, then for the civilian clothing – demob suits, as they were called – issued to returning warriors.

"Mary's (that's my poor dear wife) father had even bigger mills and the two families spent the war getting obscenely rich. She and I had been expected to make a match from the time we were born – certainly from the time it became clear that we were to have no siblings."

He went on to say that his father had foreseen the end of the good times when the war was over and had sold out at a very good price. Mary's father thought differently: he bought up all the spare capacity he could with his wartime windfall. He also bought the vast estate at the centre of which was the manor house we were sitting in.

The differences in approach by the two fathers led to a rift. Mary's father began to get rather grand ideas and came to believe that Mary could do better for herself than the Baron, plain George Stevenson in those days, who had never worked in his life and was a waster.

"I certainly didn't have enough to do. I was nominally a director of the mill but my Father wouldn't have let me pick the colour of the soap in the washroom, so I hardly even visited the place. When we sold out there was nothing left behind which I could hide my idleness!"

"Get on with the story, George, or we'll be here all night."

What the Baron did was to become a city councillor representing the Socialist party.

"The irony of a workshy youth being a Labour Councillor was not lost on my fellow party members nor on Mary's father, who wrote to me threatening to have me horsewhipped if I set foot on his estate or contacted

Mary by any means direct or indirect. The only problem was that Mary and I had fallen for each other so we had some thrilling times evading her father's vigilance to meet."

As Commonwealth countries recovered from the war, they started producing cloth at prices far below anything Britain could match. Mary's father lost everything and he was eventually forced to put the estate on the market to avoid the ignominy of bankruptcy.

Councillor George Stevenson proposed that the City Council buy the estate for the use of the public. He was howled down in the Council chamber and severely chastised in private by his party leaders – a million pounds, the asking price, would be better spent on high-rise housing for the down-trodden labourers, he was told.

His Father had died shortly after he retired leaving young George with sole control of a fortune. Rather than try to explain his ideas to the party he resigned his seat to give the council a practical demonstration: he bought the estate for himself.

When he took stock he found that about one third was profitable farming land, another third represented the house and its policies and the remainder was upland forest, grazed by sheep. The mansion needed re-roofed, re-plumbed and an introduction to the miracles of electricity. He renewed the leases on the farms and he donated the forested land to the city.

This was a master stroke, showing he had every bit as much guile as his Father. When he handed over the deeds he stressed the importance of a wilderness area for the future health of the inhabitants of the high rise urban forests.

His former colleagues on the council accepted the offer with becoming gratitude. Indeed they were so moved that they suggested the donor should be honoured with a knighthood. Now Sir George, he was able to openly court and marry Mary since his fortunes had so improved. He set about improving the part of the estate surrounding the mansion while he waited for the council to notice the snag in his largesse.

The only way for the citizens to reach their new wilderness playground was across the part of the estate still owned by Sir George! He offered to sell them the land for a road and spur railway track for one million pounds. At this stage he had spent a million, become a knighted public benefactor and was going to get his million back! Of course, he still owned almost two thirds of the original estate.

There was a lot of grumbling in the Council and not a few spiteful remarks about Sir George but they eventually agreed to pay. At this point he topped his previous masterstroke. At the eleventh hour he donated the necessary access. The Councillors, especially the ones who had been most critical of his business methods, were left looking very foolish. They proposed that he should be given a peerage.

So he got the girl, he got most of a huge estate and a peerage. Not too bad as happy endings go. He was still out one million pounds, of course, but not for long. The new road to the upland forest and an increasing population meant that he owned prime land for house building. He used the five million pounds the developers paid him so they could build affordable housing for the masses to update the mansion and the surrounding policies enabling him to live in luxury!

"I'm still a Socialist but I saw no reason to be a stupid Socialist."

Chapter Fifteen: *Taxing Times*

After our night in the baronial hall, the Laird and I parted. Driving from the island to the English Midlands had given me enough confidence in myself to accept, with little demur, that London traffic was a trial too far. I ran the Laird to the station so he could continue his journey by train and I went back to spend another night in my majestic room. I would set out, refreshed, the next morning for my return to the croft since the Laird had decided to fly back.

I parked the car behind the mansion in the old stable yard where I was almost knocked over by an old lady running across the yard pursued by a red-faced, panting nurse whose starched uniform was showing signs of wilting. The old lady was slim and upright, looking taller than she actually was because of her straight back and imperious mien.

This had to be Lady Mary and I was more than a little afraid of how she would behave. I was young and knew nothing about dementia but the word sounded as if there could be uncontrolled aggression towards strangers. There was a wild look in Lady Mary's eyes as she skidded to a halt inches from me, increasing my anxiety. Should I run or was it permissible to put her in a restraining head lock until her minder arrived?

Then she clapped her hands and her mouth lifted into a broad smile while her eyes twinkled beneath her gleaming bouffant of white hair.

"Oh look," she said, turning to the nurse, "Cousin Rupert has come to visit us!"

She took my arm and towed me through an arch into a pretty knot garden. As we walked between the manicured mini-hedges she named all the plants, although I know so little about gardening that she could have been making up the names!

She talked constantly seemingly able to breathe and speak at the same time. She asked frequent questions about my mother and sister but she never waited for a reply so I was spared the embarrassment of explaining that I had no idea what she was talking about. It was some time before I realised that she was not telling a sequential story – she would dart back and forward in time, with my, or rather Rupert's, sister married, then at school and a moment later divorced then pregnant.

Her gaiety and the relish with which she told the stories were infectious and we were still laughing and strolling in the knot garden an hour later, when the Baron and the nurse brought out coffee and cake.

"Oh look, the butler and the housekeeper are bringing out the coffee themselves. It must be footman's day off. Now what is his name? Is it Charles? No, of course not, Charles was the footman when this was daddy's house. I must be getting old! Do you think I look old?" she appealed to me with a coquettish smile.

Then she turned to her husband still standing with the tray in his hands. "What age am I now, George?"

I could see the tears in the Baron's eyes when his wife mistook him for the butler but it was much worse when the mists cleared and, for just one instant, she had recognised him.

He smiled at her and told her she was as young as she wished to be.

"In that case I am eighteen and Clarice has put my hair up for the first time and I am going to the hunt ball!"

After chattering through coffee she quickly wilted and the nurse took her indoors for a nap. She objected at first until I faithfully promised to join her for afternoon tea.

"Thank you for being so kind to her," the Baron sighed when the house door had closed behind her. "It is heart-breaking to see her like this. She had such a fine mind; such a vivid person and a wonderful conversationalist."

"But she still is a wonderful raconteur – her stories are so vivid they make you feel that you had been there when they happened."

"They are so mixed up, in her head. She used to be so well organised, never needing to take notes to remember what she had to do, not like me – I have to put everything down in my diary. She was amazing with names; she knew everyone on the estate and their children; she could remember the name and birthday of the postman and greengrocer."

"I can see that it must be hard for you but I have just met her and I am totally charmed. The pictures she paints are so full of life and it doesn't matter to me if they are out of sequence; it's as if a box of family photographs had been dropped and been put back in the wrong order."

The Baron confessed that he found it hard to spend time with her because it made him so sad but he allowed her to join us for dinner that evening. She ate very little but she had me smiling constantly, often laughing out loud, at her stories, mainly about her girlhood. Even the Baron started to look more comfortable and he occasionally risked commenting on a story or trying to jog her memory.

Lady Mary ignored him for the most part and did not respond to any of his efforts to encourage her memory but when the nurse came to fetch her at the end of the meal, she kissed her husband on the forehead and said: "Goodnight, dear."

That left him having to pretend that he had something in his eye, but after one or two trumpeting's into a handkerchief about the size of a bed sheet, he led the way into the library.

Next morning he came with me to a part of the estate I had not seen before and introduced me to the son of his forester, a strapping man well over six feet tall and with massive shoulders.

"Wilfred has got a job with the Forestry Commission in Scotland. Bright boy, he got a first at agricultural college. I thought you could give him a lift to Spean Bridge. Company for you on the journey, what?"

Once we had learned to slow our speech to make us intelligible to each other we got on very well. I was keen on sub atomic physics where the action lasts for fractions of a second while his love was plants that would not reach maturity in his lifetime. I think he was as surprised as I was that there was so much common ground between our two preoccupations.

He stayed in my room in Glasgow that night, reluctantly taking my bed while I camped out in a sleeping bag on the cushions from the settee laid on the floor. In the end he accepted that his longer body would have overlapped the cushions so it made sense for him to take the bed. It was a reality check for me: two nights in a luxurious room in a mansion then a sleeping bag and scratchy cushions!

After I dropped Wilfred off I had still about seventy miles to drive with nothing to do but think. The Laird had had the car radio removed in case it distracted him from his driving! Since I had started driving I had begun to notice the condition of roads. Especially on this long trip I had noticed the different road surfaces and the noise the tyres made on them. I remembered that many of the roads on the journey between the island and Glasgow had potholes and crumbling verges. Even the minor roads around the Baron's estate were poorly maintained.

At this point, I metaphorically sat up: the island roads have no potholes, well-tended verges and unblemished surfaces. Even the city streets around my home are in poorer condition.

"It's all because of the two hikers," Uncle James enlightened me. Well, not 'enlightened' exactly since I could see no connection between potholes and walkers. Not that I any longer expected a story of James' to be straightforward!

"The roads were just awful before they came. Great holes in them that would have swallowed a mini without trace. Gashes a foot wide where an overflowing burn had washed away everything to a depth of two feet."

It became so bad that the locals started leaving their decent vehicles in the ferry car park on the mainland. The only powered transport they would use on the island was tractors and broken down old vans and trucks that could not get much worse by dropping into chasms.

The hikers arrived one autumn near the end of the tourist season. They were polite young Englishmen who walked the whole length of the island, being spoiled by the landladies of the bed and breakfast houses they stayed at.

"They look awful peaky. It's the bad air down in London but they're getting a bit of colour in their cheeks since they arrived." It turned out that it was probably embarrassment that brought the red to their cheeks.

"I just put a few more rashers of bacon on their plates – they need feeding up. Maybe an extra sausage and eggs cost next to nothing with the hens laying so well."

The only things that marked them out from the hundreds of other hikers that came and went over the years were the clipboards. They walked the roads in their shorts and hiking boots with their back packs on their shoulders but everywhere they went they made wee notes on their clipboards.

Speculation was rife. Were they archaeologists planning a dig to uncover Viking relics? Or, perhaps, they were researching a travel book. There was some concern that they were anthropologists taking notes of the peculiar habits of the natives so they could write us up like Lillian Beckwith did in Skye.

What they actually were was inspectors from the Highways Agency and the notes they were taking were about the road tax discs on the island motor vehicles. The islanders had long since stopped paying road tax on anything that was driven only on the island. The cars in the ferry car park were all fully licensed and insured but the old bangers were left untaxed. Even the Minister's Ford Anglia, which should really have been in a museum, had a tax disc that was ten years out of date! The ultimate embarrassment was that Lachlan's official police land rover did not have a valid tax disc!

The letters started to arrive a week after the hikers left containing threats of huge fines, even imprisonment. It would have wrecked the island's fragile economy and clearly some accommodation would have to be found. The Treasury and the Scottish Office set up an ad hoc (and totally secret) working group that deliberated in Whitehall for nearly six months.

"In the end they charged us all six months back tax and promised to improve the roads. We had a team of men and a road roller on the island for the best part of a year so the bed and breakfast folk got back more than they invested in the hikers!"

Chapter Sixteen: *Venus Arising from the Radox*

When I first started visiting the island, Aunt Effie put me in a wee box room at the top of the stairs in the croft house. James' Grandfather had built a two-storey, stone house to replace the old thatched black house. It became the byre with corrugated iron replacing the rushes when the thatch finally rotted.

The house had two good sized bedrooms upstairs, camceiled with walls panelled in tongue and groove pine. The box room lay between the bedrooms with a skylight and space for a single bed and a little chest of drawers that doubled as a bedside table. At the bottom of the stairs there was a porch that held the outdoor clothing and footwear. There was a room off the porch with a fireplace that was used when the Minister called: the Laird used to be ushered in there until he objected to the frigid formality and insisted on joining us in the family room.

This room was the centre of our life. We dined off the table and sat afterwards on a two-seater settee or a comfy armchair standing sentry so that the peat fire could not escape without surrendering its heat. Beyond the table was a door into the kitchen; I do not remember that door ever being closed. The kitchen had a calor gas oven and hob and a sink. Beyond the kitchen was an extension that housed the toilet and bathroom; it, like everything else on the island, had its own history.

Before there was either running water or drainage, water was brought from the well. When you had washed the dishes or shaved you opened the kitchen window and threw the water out into a soak away that

James had constructed when he came home from the Navy. Then he put in drainage pipes to a septic tank behind the old byre and built the extension with a ceramic toilet and a cast iron bath.

At first there was this gleaming white cistern but no water: a bucket of water was left beside the pan except when the Minister called when the bucket was emptied into the cistern. He was a gentle, diffident man but he had reached the age where he had to pee at every stop. Half way through his cup of tea he would blush:

"Would you very much mind, Effie my dear, if I availed myself of your ...er.. facilities?"

About two years later, a grant from the bureaucrats in Brussels allowed the council to put in main drainage. The septic tank was emptied for the last time and left uncovered while James decided how he could redeploy it. Not untypically it was a further five years before mains water was supplied. At this point the extension became a functional but drafty bathroom. Aunt Effie hated it!

By the time I started visiting the island, the locals had started to by-pass the middle men, exporting on their own behalf. Uncle James exported lobsters and crabs to gourmet restaurants in France and Spain. He had his own label - Island Fisheries . Hamish collected the packages, put them into custom built containers and saw them loaded onto charter flights. He spoke good Spanish and more than passable French so the islanders left it to him to negotiate the contracts.

With the extra cash coming in and a timely improvement grant, Uncle James built a new, timber-framed byre with a tiled roof and shingled walls. The black house, still structurally sound, was relegated once more and became an oubliette for damaged creels, broken wheels, odd oars and pretty well every other kind of jetsam that accumulated about a working croft. It was an Aladdin's cave with a distinctive tarry, sea weedy smell. Aunt Effie reluctantly accepted that a new bathroom would have to wait.

The year I started University I arrived at the croft just as Hamish pulled away in his van. Apart from transporting sea food and wheeler-dealing with foreigners, he fitted kitchens and bathrooms – his nickname was Hamish Toilet, or Lavvy, or other less acceptable synonyms.

To my utter horror, I found that my wonderful wee box room had been given a dormer window and fitted with a brand new bathroom suite complete with pedestal washbasin and boxed-in bath!

Aunt Effie was waiting at the bottom of the stairs with her face glowing, clearly waiting for me to go into raptures over the 'improvement'.

"Where am I supposed to sleep?" was the best I could muster. Even as I said it I could have cut my tongue out. James and Effie had done so much for me over the years. Now they had a facility that we took for granted in the city but was a luxury to them and all I could do was moan about what would happen to me.

I looked at Effie thinking she would be offended but her face was still glowing and she failed to supress what, in anyone else, I would have called a giggle.

"You'll have to see your Uncle James about that. He's out in the old byre."

My first thought was that she could have been more sympathetic, after all I had regretted what I had said about the new bathroom, hadn't I? I began to feel a bit petulant again so I stomped off round the new byre with its aluminium double doors allowing access to the tractor and round the corner to the black house. I was a bit surprised to find that Effie was coming with me. She had to break into a little run every so often when my longer strides threatened to carry me away but she managed to be on my heels when the old house came in view. She usually only came down this far to milk the cow or get some tatties from the clamp.

I stopped so suddenly that she bumped into me. Facing me was Uncle James inside a transformed black house, lately byre. He was leaning on the bottom half of a stable door set in new architraves quietly smoking his pipe. The outside of the house was newly rendered and white-washed a dazzling white. The two windows, that had been boarded up as long as I could remember, were newly glazed.

"I see your admiring the wall. It's some new-fangled plastic sealing that keeps out even the island weather: guaranteed for twenty years."

Above his head, the rusting corrugated iron on the roof had been replaced with dusky red felt tiles surrounding what were unmistakeably, but unbelievably, solar panels. James knocked out his pipe, stepped back and opened the bottom half of the door.

"*Thig a staigh*. Since you seem to have made the island your second home, we thought you should have a place of your own. Welcome to your new home."

It was a palace in miniature. What had been a dirt floor was now polished hardwood. The fireplace had been repointed and there were flowers in a vase on the mahogany mantelpiece that was also new. To the right was a door into a kitchen to the front and a shower room with toilet to the back.

But it was the bedroom that took my breath away. At the back of the house, above the bed, the roof was entirely of glass like a conservatory. I would be able to lie in bed at night and look up into the infinity of the stars!

"We put a wheen of them solar panels in so there should be plenty hot water both here and in the big house. It seemed to me that sunlight in the island was more so-little than so-lar but Hamish tells me there should be no problem. The shower is there because you have probably discovered girls and started to care about your personal hygiene."

How do the islanders know these things? Of course I had had crushes but not a twinge of my heartstrings – until today. One of my big crushes was Morag who worked as a waitress for Gran in the holidays. She was on the platform at Queen Street today and we had travelled back together. She was completing her doctorate of philosophy but, as usual, she talked to me, a mere fresher, like an equal.

I have found that it is difficult to maintain lust for someone who treats you like a brother: it somehow seems a bit naff to picture her in a bikini or less when she is talking to you as an intelligent grown up. We found plenty to talk about on the journey and we were still chatting when we got off the train for the ferry trip to the island. Suddenly she looked over my shoulder and her face lit up. I wished someone would look at me in that way!

I dragged out our bags then turned to see her hugging and dancing with another redhead. When they turned to me, Morag started to introduce us but, before she could say the first word, I fell in love.

"This is Flora, my brat of a sister and this..."

"Oh I know who he is. It's the geek that keeps trying to look down your blouse at his Gran's tearoom."

'Crestfallen' is a word I had heard but I suddenly understood its full impact. I had been polishing phrases in my mind that would make her see me in a good light, perhaps even win her friendship if not her affection, and she had crushed me with a sentence.

Morag looked a bit put out and she started to say something but Flora stepped forward put her hands on my shoulders and air-kissed close to my left ear. So quietly that only I could hear, she whispered:

"You can look down my cleavage any time!"

I went from eunuch to rampant stallion in a heartbeat!

That was the start of a magical summer. Flora and I were together as often as we possibly could, falling deeper and deeper into a love that was perfectly matched. I am not going to tell you about it. If you were ever eighteen and in love you know, and no words of mine can equal the magic of your remembrances. If it never happened to you, I pity you, but I still could not find the words to describe the whirlwind kaleidoscope of elation and despair, hope and fear, the fallings out and the reconciliations.

Written down it would sound trite – even tacky – but when you are living it, living the exploration of another person's body and soul there is a magic beyond any other human emotion.

If Uncle James did guess on that day at the transformed black house it was only hours before the whole island was in the secret. There may have been some of the old cailleachs who disapproved but everyone we met seemed to smile on us indulgently. Flora and I felt that people approved of us!

Not only did I fall in love but it was on that summer holiday that I first saw a grown woman totally naked. It was not in the slightest degree an erotic experience and it was the result of fitting a new window in the bathroom.

Aunt Effie really enjoyed her new bath. She would rush to finish her chores in the morning and then, before she started cooking the dinner, she would collect her library book from beside her bed and a fresh warm towel then retreat to the bath.

More than once she complained of a buzzing noise when she was lying there. Uncle James never heard anything when he was in the bath but then he spent most of his time singing Gaelic songs at the top of his voice. I had my own shower but I went and listened lying in the dry bath to please my Aunt but I could only hear the normal sounds of croft life.

Hamish Toilet came, tapped the walls, shook the pipes and said he thought he might, just possibly, hear next to nothing. It sounded more like a bagpipe drone to him than a buzzing: Effie told him he was havering so he went away in a huff telling James that it would just be the pipes settling down.

The buzzing got louder as the summer wore on and in the end we all heard it. We even had a conference about the noise with Aunt Effie, Uncle James, Flora and I all crushed into the little room listening intently.

"If it was outside, I would have said it was bees," James mused, almost prophetically.

When the bath was put in, the skylight was replaced by a dormer window and the wall was made good with plaster board. It was all exposed during that first summer and the plan was to tile the bottom half and paper the upper walls during the winter.

One afternoon the Laird had come over to discuss something with Uncle James and they were standing at the gable end of the house looking up at the wall. I had been sitting dreaming of Flora but I went over to join them, having become intrigued by two grown men standing looking at a blank, and very ordinary, wall.

Aunt Effie was in the bath as usual at that time and it was one of those rare afternoons when the air was so still you could almost hear the flapping of a butterfly's wings.

Suddenly there was a piercing shriek and a commotion from the house. The buzzing turned out to be wasps that had been using the plaster board to fortify their bike and they had broken through into the room more angry than repentant.

Effie, showing a commendable turn of speed, was out of the bathroom without even waiting to snatch up the towel. In a state of nature she was downstairs and out the house, and if she couldn't outrun a speeding bullet she certainly outdistanced a tail of irate insects.

She must have thought James was in the new byre for she rushed past yelling his name not noticing the three of us standing puzzled within touching distance. There was a moment's stunned silence after she passed. Then the Laird, ever the gentleman, turned to James.

"Was that a new frock Effie had on? I don't think I've seen her in it before."

"Man, I couldn't tell you, but it would have looked better if she had run the iron over it to get out some of the wrinkles."

Chapter Seventeen: *Blind Drunk*

Uncle James and I were out in the minch again, sitting in a triangulated position that placed us above a rock where whiting congregated. The water was not deep but we could not set an anchor since it would have disturbed the fish. I was giving an occasional dab with the oars to keep us in position.

"My Father was still alive when I left the Navy and him and me settled back into our old ways. He was as proud as could be of my rank and my medals, although the only person he ever told was my Mother. The trouble is that he still treated me like a ten year old, ordering me about and giving me only the most menial jobs."

I was keenly aware that two privileges were being extended to me. The location of whiting rocks is a closely guarded secret passed down through the generations! Uncle James had got the hand lines out and was baiting the hooks with lug worm that we had dug up at low tide. They shared the sandy beach with cockles and we had collected them too, leaving them in a bucket of salt water so they would flush out the grit. I felt even more favoured when he began, without prompting, to tell me more of his history.

"Keep the left hand chimney of Alan Beag's house exactly in front of thon double pylon; and hold her where you can just see the pillar box keeking out behind the hotel."

He had got the lines out and his pipe drawing well before he answered my question about what he did after he left the Royal Navy at the end of the Falkland's war.

"It was only a matter of time before my father or I attempted murder of the other so I took myself off to Aberdeen and signed on as First Mate on a vessel supplying the oil rigs. I had got my merchant seaman's certificates while I was in the service; in fact I missed out on the first job I applied for because I had a Master's qualification."

James had applied for the post of deck hand on the island ferry only to be told he was over-qualified. They kept his application on their files, however, and eighteen months later he became mate of a Macbrayne boat sailing out of Oban. He came back to run the croft when his father broke his hip while carrying hay to the byre and endured his advice and criticism until the old man died.

"The Navy is famous for its spit and polish: on the supply boat they spat freely enough but the very most they would do was to rub it into the deck with their feet! I was about the fourth or fifth First Mate they had had in as many months."

It all stemmed, it seemed, from the captain, who drank not less than a bottle of spirits a day and was too drunk by ten in the morning to take any part in the running of a boat: "He would have struggled to steer a fork to his own mouth," as James explained. So the handling of vessel and crew devolved on the First Mate. The crew were rough and paid far less than the men working on the offshore rigs.

Aberdeen was a mecca for the dross of the Scottish central belt. Coaches lined up outside Saughton, Barlinnie and Peterhead to take released prisoners to join the other prospectors for black gold.

After every voyage, the better sailors drew their pay and joined an oil company operating in the North Sea. The work was not so hard, the pay was better and they had long breaks on shore. They were replaced by the unemployable dregs of a boom town. You have seen movies about the lawless west of the United States: Aberdeen and Peterhead were the Wild East!

It was the task of the First Mate to make seamen of them, at least to the point where the only life they endangered was their own. Most had never known discipline except when serving time in prison and they all resented attempts to steer them into the paths of duty.

Most of the First Mates left after one voyage – one even hailed the pilot boat on the way out of harbour and was taken ashore before the boat left port in fear of his life! Some of the mates drank with the captain and let the crew get on with things: making a kirk or a mill of it, as my Gran says. Some sided with the men and tried to coax them into obedience, but nothing worked.

"I was lucky. I signed on when they had just docked after surviving a storm by the grace of God and the seamanship of the boatswain, who was the only officer sober when the gale hit them. Sick and staring death in the face, they understood, perhaps for the first time, the value of training and discipline."

There had been a bit of a setback to the price of oil so most of the crew remained with the boat. They had been frightened witless and appreciated the need for trained cooperation, so they grumbled but accepted the regime Uncle James initiated. The man on the wheel summed it up on their first night at sea.

"See you, Jamsie, you're aw righ'. At least you ken which end o' the boat goes first. You're a hard man but none the war o' that. Just remember that this is no' the Royal bloody Navy!"

"In its own way, that meant more to me than the medal citation."

They made it to the rig, unloaded their supplies and stood off in support until they were relieved. They would normally have returned to port as soon as they unloaded but the oil company decided to save money by using them as a guard boat. It was almost the death of the captain because the vodka ran out the day before they docked.

The crew were less sullen and argumentative since they knew what was expected of them. James praised them when they got things right and bawled them out the rest of the time. They still grumbled but in a less whole-hearted way than they had in the past.

When they got into port they were sent to an old pier while they waited for their usual loading berth to come free. It was no further from the pubs than their usual pitch but the pier had no more than three lights along its length to help them negotiate the usual clutter of hawsers and crates. The old boatswain and James agreed to be the duty watch so the rest of the crew, officers and men, could go ashore for a bevvy.

Paying off was complicated since most of the crew had deductions, some voluntary to wives back in Glasgow and Edinburgh, but most enforced by law to cover unpaid fines, child support and loan sharks. Many of the newcomers lacked papers and were on emergency tax code. The pay was dealt with by the captain's wife who would come aboard in the morning to do the PAYE and re-stock the liquor cabinet with several crates of ardent spirits.

James was allowed to advance up to a quarter of the anticipated pay when they reached port which gave the crew enough to get bluttered but not enough for fatal alcohol poisoning. Falling off the dock on the way back to the boat was another matter!

The crew started returning after Uncle James' first voyage shortly after midnight. They were all drunk after their natures – some argumentative, some belligerent, some merry and some stopping every few yards to vomit up a little more of the evening's intake of beer and spirits. Half and half was the fashionable drink of the cognoscenti: a gill of whisky washed down with a half pint of heavy ale. The tide had been dropping since they tied up so the deck was now about three metres below the dock. A vertical iron ladder connected the two with the lower rungs still wet and slick with weed.

The more experienced sailors negotiated the ladder with a certain drunken élan but James and the boatswain stood by on the deck to offer what assistance they could. All went moderately smoothly, although the peace of the neighbourhood was lost in volleys of oaths, until a city boy on his first trip got to the top of the ladder. He was no more drunk than the rest but his previous sea-going time had been confined to the Govan Ferry.

He missed his footing near the top and slid the rest of the way down with the sides of the ladder running through his hands. At each step his head banged against the rung and he landed on the deck in a welter of blood. He remained conscious and danced around the deck complaining about the pain in his hands that had been rubbed raw. When James reached him he was struggling to breathe through the blood and snot running into his mouth, spitting it out, gasping for breath and then cursing until he had to go through the whole process again.

"Will some o' you bastards turn the lights back on? A canny see a thing." He gasped through a spray of blood and saliva. When he was assured that the lights were on his voice dropped to a panicky whisper.

"Oh my God. Am blind. A canny see!"

An ambulance arrived with commendable speed and took him to the infirmary with Uncle James in attendance. He was taken straight into an operating theatre while James paced about the waiting area wondering if there was anything he could have done to prevent the tragedy. He was wondering if he could have rigged lines to help the men down and he had started to compose a letter to the man's partner when the surgeon came out of the operating theatre grinning.

"I hope this means good news and that the poor lad is not going to lose his sight." Uncle James was a bit frosty since he felt that the grin was inappropriate in the tragic circumstances.

"His sight is as good as yours or mine. He doesn't even have concussion. His hands will take about a week to heal but otherwise he's in better shape than he deserves. They do say that God looks after fools and drunks and he is both.

"What happened was that the iron rungs sliced his head and a flap of scalp came loose and fell over his eyes; I stitched it back and he'll be as good as new when he sobers up."

That was why he couldn't see: he was blinded by his own hair still firmly attached to the underlying skin! So, just as in the Wild West, scalping came to the Wild East.

Chapter Eighteen: *Turning the Clock Back*

I was brought up in the Church of Scotland but we were never a very religious family. We went to church at Easter, sometimes at Christmas but it was no big deal: if you did not want to attend neither my Mum nor Dad would make an issue of it. On the island it was a different story – they take church attendance very seriously indeed.

Flora's parents liked me and they approved of my family. They kept stressing that we were too young to know our own minds but they made no objection to us seeing each other whenever our chores allowed. Flora and Morag, when she was at home, went to morning service every Sunday and their parents started to make pointed remarks about my non-attendance. Since I did not have strong feelings either way, I started going to church.

It was no epiphany: the only way I could spend time with Flora on Sunday morning was to be in church. Of course, I could not sit beside her in their family pew. I had to take a place in Uncle James' pew that, fortunately, was near the back so I could not only watch Flora throughout the service; I could also hide my total ignorance of the order of service and when to stand and sit.

Members of the congregation leased a pew for the year and woe betides anyone who sat in the wrong place. In some churches the main task of the sidemen is to take the collection but on the island they were watchdogs steering casual visitors into safe seats where they could participate without giving offence. I did sometimes wonder how God felt about this territorial terrorism.

I quite enjoyed going to church as it turned out. There is something satisfying about having your conscience opened to the inspection of the gimlet eye of a minister in black gown and Geneva bands. I imagined that my life must be full of sins, most of them totally beyond my knowledge and many beyond my control. As Shakespeare might have said: 'there are more sins on heaven and earth than are dreamt of in your philosophy.' I thought of it the way you do about walking under a ladder: not a smart thing to do but you just sigh with relief if you get away with it and go forth to sin again.

I even delved into the New Testament where I discovered that Jesus preached inclusion and love. I concluded that this message had somehow evaded the Church of Scotland. The island people do actually live pretty close to Christian principles; they share chores, help their neighbours and they are tolerant of each other. They are more likely to smile than to take offence if you upset them. I do not know if this arises from natural sweetness of temper or generations of Hellfire preaching.

The bonus from my attendance was that I was allowed to walk home with Flora. We would dawdle on the way, holding hands and talking about everything in the World until it was time for Sunday dinner. We worked on a three week cycle going to Flora's house one week, James and Effie the next and to my Gran's on the third week. During the tourist season the tearoom was open so instead of dinner we had Sunday supper when we ate in Gran's flat above the shop.

Very often, Flora would be waitressing so I mooched around the town like a wraith until she came off duty with her pockets clinking with tips. Then, while Gran prepared the meal, Flora and I would stand at the window looking over the harbour with our hands just touching or she would put her foot over mine and give it a little squeeze. We never made open contact with each other in any of the houses. I do not think anyone would have disapproved but they would have commented and, most probably, teased us.

Certainly Gran turned out to be a hopeless romantic and any sign of affection would have had her making wedding favours. It is odd that while she was the only one of the adults who had married fairly late, she was the only one who thought that Flora and I would stay together for life. Whichever house we went to, the older folk settled down after dinner to read the papers or to watch television so we would slip out and have yet another long walk. We never seemed to run out of things to say; it was just so natural to tell her all my hopes and fears for the future. There was absolutely no doubt in our minds that we would be together for always.

Once the flow of tourists slackened we had to change the routine when we ate at Gran's flat. She took no Sunday papers and she watched nothing on television except the news. What she enjoyed was asking forthright questions that would have us blushing and squirming in our seats. She could be outrageous on any subject, but her favourite theme was that we had things much easier than when she was our age.

One day, I made the mistake of complaining that Flora's parents wanted her in before midnight on a Saturday.

"The dance doesn't finish until quarter to twelve so we hardly have time for a wee chat on the way home."

"By 'a wee chat' I take it you mean a big snog," replied Gran with her customary tact. "It always amazes me that you two can chat with your arms that tight about each other that you can hardly breathe and your lips glued together!"

"That's uncalled for, Gran!" I could be a pompous nerd when I got embarrassed. "I freely admit that I might do what you said but Flora is a very well brought up girl."

"Wheesht, lad. Even the Queen has had a wee snog in her day and she is as well brought up as it's possible to be.

"You're lucky Flora's folks give you until midnight. When I was a lass the Sabbath started at eleven thirty on Saturday night. We wouldn't even have been able to have the last dance."

Her Father had been very strict in his observance of Sunday as a day of rest. The only work that was allowed was tending the animals. Even the meals were taken cold and had to be prepared the evening before to minimise the work done on Sunday. Her Mother was only able to have a cup of tea when she boiled the kettle for the mealy mash prepared for the dogs. Gran's Father considered this a major concession and he was troubled that it might jeopardise his chances in Heaven.

He was a lay preacher who delivered a sermon in Gaelic every Sunday at two o'clock. The ordained minister took to the pulpit at eleven on the Sabbath morning and had his congregation out the door by ten past twelve at the latest. Her Father showed no such consideration. Gaelic is a lovely lilting language, flowing smoothly almost without plosives but delivered in a sombre baritone lacking inflection except when calling down retribution on sinners, it can be very dreary – dreich is the word.

The church had a fine organ but it was replaced in the Gaelic service by a presenter who droned out the metric psalms line by weary line. The whole service lasted never less than two hours and had been known to exceed three!

"I used to sit there wishing the General Assembly of the Church of Scotland would declare that preaching was work and ban it on a Sunday," Gran said. "Of course, we had to go every Sunday – and stay awake and alert the whole time. Father would often question us about the sermon on the way back to the croft."

"So, if you had to be in by eleven thirty you would have had to leave the dance by eleven to get home on time – no wee cuddles for you, eh Gran!"

She gave a sly little smile.

"Where there's a will there's a way," and she tapped her nose with her index finger.

"C'mon, Gran, stop being mysterious and just tell us what you did."

"Well, my Father worked very hard and most nights he went up to bed before ten. On a Saturday, while we were out, Mother heated water for him to have his bath in the tin tub in front of the fire. He had first use of the water and she would follow him into the tub while he got dressed as close as possible to the fire. Then he sat by the fire reading his Gaelic bible until we got home. He wasn't checking up on us exactly for he liked to start the Sabbath on the stroke of midnight with a family prayer and a wee reading from the good book.

"He would be settled by nine in front of a fire well banked up so it would keep the house reasonably warm the next day when it had to be allowed to go out. By ten he had nodded off in the chair and he would then sleep until he heard us at the door. As soon as he was gently snoring, my Mother would put the clock back by an hour.

"When we arrived home, the first thing my father would do was to look at the clock that read exactly eleven thirty. Every week he would turn to my mother, point out the time and tell her how blessed they were to have such obedient children. My Mother was always up first in the morning so she just put the clock forward again and he was never any the wiser!"

Chapter Nineteen: *The Other Flora: Fauna Also*

The new cow started to follow me around the croft. Although James had only had her for two years, after the old cow died, she was allowed to roam free, never straying far and always outside the byre morning and evening to be milked. At first she tagged along at a discrete distance but by the third day she was on my heels, lowing pitifully and butting me in the back with her head.

"Time she had a social visit to the bull," Uncle James said. "Would you travel with her in the horse box – she's a nervous passenger but she'll be fine on the way back."

The bull was communal property cared for at various crofts according to a complex and jealously applied rota; like many things on the island that appeared random, even chaotic, to outsiders it was governed by a strictly observed set of rules. At the moment he was housed with Hamish Kitchen on the far side of the island.

"Why was she following me around, pushing me and moaning?"

"It's because cows are basically stupid creatures. The man I bought her from called the vet when a cow came into season and he artificially inseminated them with a syringe. That dazzlingly white shirt you have taken to wearing since you met Flora must have looked like the white coat the vet wears. I don't want to be indelicate, but the old cow took a fancy to have you as her next mate! I think if we had left her another day she might have jumped on your back to get your attention."

We were standing watching the bull mounted on the skinny rump of the lovesick beast. Hamish was at work, but his wife had brought us out cups of tea and a homemade sponge cake filled with raspberry jam and lashings of cream.

"I thought sheep were supposed to be the stupid animals."

"They are not altogether wise, I will admit, but they are doctors of philosophy compared to cattle. In fact, sheep are a lot like people: they have their own favourite places; they have irrational panics and run about aimlessly in groups.

"I have heard people from cities say that all sheep look alike but their faces are quite distinctive. When I was young we ran about five hundred sheep and I knew them all – and I had a name for each of them. Perhaps they are smarter than humans because I have never met a sheep that could not distinguish between people!"

"How do you find names for five hundred sheep?"

"Well, I gave them the names of people I knew – the sheep I didn't like I called after old cailleachs, or the Minister. If I liked the beast I would name it after a friend who reminded me of that particular sheep. I sometimes changed the name of a sheep if I fell out with someone.

"When we gathered the sheep in the autumn for clipping and dipping, I would know where to look for every ewe. Of course, I was young and would become distracted by my thoughts but my dog would keep me right if I missed one!

"All the crofters helped with the clipping and dipping. One croft would gather the sheep to the fank, which was usually shared by all the crofts in the township. The most experienced men had specialist duties and the rest of us brought the sheep to them.

"The teenage boys would bring forward a ewe to the clipper who would turn the beast on her back and take the fleece off in one piece, starting at the neck. Next the feet were inspected for rot and the tail for maggots. Damaged hoofs were pared until they began to bleed and were then disinfected with Stockholm tar. After that they were put into the tank of dip and released onto the hillside where they would stand for a minute or two bawling at the indignity before they started cropping the grass and wandered back home along the well-trodden sheep tracks.

"The cut fleece was taken to a shed and inspected. If it was decently clean it was rolled and put into a sack hanging from the roof. It was about three metres deep and held a small boy who tramped down the fleeces so the bag was completely filled.

"It was a scary job. When you were dropped into the sack by one of the men, the hessian walls stretched away above your head. The fleeces came flying in at you and would knock you off balance especially as a pile of wool is not a very stable platform to stand on. I remember the relief when my head finally came out the neck of the sack and I could see all the activity. I felt that I had been in a smelly dungeon. It had its compensations: even in the coldest weather your hands never got cold because of all the lanolin in the wool."

The autumn clip was also the time when the male lambs lost their testicles. An instrument spread a strong elastic band and then released it just where the scrotum joined the body. With the blood supply cut off the sack withered and eventually dropped off with the wound already healed.

"In the old days they used to lib the lambs, as they called it, with a sharp knife. The crofter held the scrotum in one hand and cut the sack with the knife in the other hand; he would then lean forward and use his teeth to pull out the testicles!"

Uncle James thought that the domestic animals were the really clever ones. "Cats despise us but they also despise themselves for enjoying our company! If they become fond of you they will bring you presents of mice or birds – even baby rabbits. Of course if they are hungry they will eat everything but the choice bits, like the heart, that they will leave as a tribute on your doorstep."

He thought dogs were the smartest of all with the possible exception of pigs. "Dogs know they are cleverer than us and they feel responsible for keeping us out of harm's way. They cannot figure out why it takes us so long to get from sleep to the hillside. They have a fur coat and hard pads with claws to give them purchase on slippery ground while we have to put on clothes and boots to venture out. I think they pity us for having only two feet when four are obviously more practical."

By this time the bull had recovered from his first exertion and was mounted again to the obvious satisfaction of the cow. James watched this coupling very carefully and pronounced himself satisfied that the mating would be fruitful; "if the poor girl still has it in her", he added.

"I have been reading about these 'same sex couples', as they call them, are having babies by artificial insemination and I wondered whether they would get like the cow and get all excited – 'horny' is the word they use, I think – when they see a stethoscope around someone's neck."

The island has far more wild country than cultivated ground. The best land in the townships is divided amongst the crofts where it is planted with potatoes and oats; the rest is hill pasture or marsh with an abundant freckling of rocks. Walking home from the shore at the gloaming through the bog myrtle pleasantly assaults the sense of smell and provokes assaults of a less pleasant kind by the clouds of midges that rise solid as a black cloak at every step. In the machair there are small, pretty orchids and, waving above the coarse grass, the heads of bog cotton flutter in the breeze.

Higher up bracken and heather take control. Pigs have a taste for the succulent roots of bracken and help to limit the encroachment. The snout of a pig could root out iron bars and they are equipped with formidable teeth. They can be bad-tempered and are not to be trusted – they are one of the few animals that will attack the person who regularly feeds them.

Walking through heather is very tiring – and painfully scratchy if you are wearing shorts! The best way to deal with crossing a patch of heather is to hop, a bit like athletes do in the triple jump. That way the springiness of the heather propels you forward, especially if you do it at speed. Uncle James told me that it was possible to catch grouse by leaping through the ling in this way so I spent several days trying it for myself when I was about fifteen – young and daft!

The grouse is a heavy bird and, when startled, it will only fly a short distance. At the first alarm the birds might fly two hundred metres but the distance gets shorter as they begin to tire. James' story was that a young lad – me! – runs at the grouse and keeps on running never allowing them time to recover before they are forced to fly again. After some hours the grouse will be so exhausted that they will stagger into a game bag held open for them! All I have to report is that either grouse are much fitter than they used to be or I am a wimp! I never did get closer than a hundred metres before collapsing in the heather with my lungs on fire and my legs like jelly.

The other bird that outwits man is the hooded crow. The body is grey with black head and wings. They are reputed to attack lambs and the result is particularly horrific since they only go for the eyes, clearly a delicacy in hoodies cuisine. Experts say that the birds only disfigure lambs already dead but the crofters are not convinced.

The birds can certainly identify quite subtle differences in people. Walk over the hills with a stick the size and approximate shape of a shotgun and the hoodies will move just enough to keep them out of range of your boot. Carry a real shotgun and the sky will be clear of crows before you have moved ten paces.

Uncle James was amused by my interest in the natural history of the island but I think that he was pleased at the same time. He certainly took a lot of time to show me things that I would have missed. He knocked a limpet from a rock, brushed off the flesh and rinsed the fleshy sole in a rock pool. It proved to be a sort of salty chewing gum. It is a very gristly muscle strong enough to hold the animal on a rock during the most severe gales. After about half an hour of chewing it begins to break up presumably when your saliva starts to digest it.

Just as on land where sausages, haggis and black pudding ensure that no part of the animal is wasted, so with fish. During the season mackerel almost throw themselves into the boat when they frenziedly feed on herring fry. I have caught more than a hundred on a still evening. They follow the fry to the surface then flip over slapping the water with their tails. It sounds just like clapping, and it is eerie to sit in a dinghy killing fish while you are being applauded by their fellows. On shore the mackerel are gutted and hung in pairs over a plank in the sunshine where they kipper in their own oil. A liberal sprinkling of black pepper discourages the flies.

One of James' favourite meals was made by scraping the brains from a cod head, mixing them with seasoned oatmeal and returning the mixture to the fish head. The mess is boiled and eaten with gusto – by Uncle James! I have had a forkful within ten centimetres of my mouth, at which point my stomach heaved so hard that I had to concentrate my whole will on keeping the contents down!

Chapter Twenty: *Monkey Business*

When I was still at school my visits to the island had coincided with the tourist season. The longer holidays I enjoyed now I was at university, meant that I could linger after the coaches joined the martins and swallows on the road south. One real surprise was my first experience of a proper ceilidh.

They held ceilidhs two or three times a week in the hotels during the summer when an act from Inverness or Edinburgh would perform. Backing would come from an accordion and fiddle while a piper would grace the occasion – usually out of doors so as not to offend sensitive Sassenach ears. The players were usually incomers and supplemented their meagre earnings at the show by tending bar or cleaning holiday cottages. The audiences at these gatherings sat in rows and, for the most part, clapped politely although as the evening wore on and the bar receipts mounted, a few would take to the aisles in a confident but inept parody of Highland dancing.

The real ceilidh had much more in common with a church social in the urban central belt. The big urn in the village hall would be filled with water and put on to boil by four o'clock. Sandwiches and cakes would be set out on trestle tables by the ladies who had donated them. As usual on the island there was a strict order, a rigid hierarchy, that you ignored at your peril. Gran and Effie had by far the best tearoom on the island but only Effie was allowed to put cakes on the top table. Gran, as a returning native, was relegated to table two. Flora, because of her age, had to exhibit under her Mother's name!

One team of helpers from the senior classes in the Academy, made gallons of squash for the kids while another team, made up of middle-aged ladies, filled and refilled enormous aluminium kettles that must have held a gallon of strong, stewed tea. After years of acrimonious debate, they had only just stopped adding sugar to the tea at source. At the suggestion of the Minister, an experienced and wily diplomat, they had put sugar in some but not in all the kettles. While sound in principle the idea had to be abandoned because by the time refills were being brought round no one could remember which kettles were sugared.

The entertainment was provided by local talent, which was considerable. One matron, trained in the Royal College of Music, had played in concert halls throughout the World. Now she was content to entertain her neighbours with heart-stoppingly beautiful music on the clarsach. Youngsters got up to cover current chart hits and they were followed by grannies singing waulking songs they had learned from their grannies. Then there were a few songs from a girl who performed regularly on BBC Alba. She arrived late because she had been on duty at the Cottage Hospital.

After the tea and cakes had been cleared away the chairs were put back against the walls so the young folk could dance. The older people sat contentedly watching and enjoying a *ceilidh* – the word just means a chat. Two accordions, a double bass and a drum kit provided the music. The fiddler who played in the hotels usually appeared but this particular night he was busy doing his other job of sous-chef for a party of anglers.

The highlight of this, the first ceilidh I attended, was my Uncle James singing a comic song in Gaelic about an islander who brought a monkey home from Africa. Although I was trying to learn Gaelic, I missed most of the humour but James' antics had me laughing along with the men who roared approval while the women tutted audibly and hid their giggles behind their hands. Purely comic Gaelic songs are rare but funny, not to mention scurrilous, words are often set to popular Gaelic tunes.

In the old days a team of eight men would row ten miles or so to the mainland to fetch supplies. Outbound they ballasted the boat with rocks that were replaced by sacks of oatmeal, salt and other necessities. To keep time they would sing songs that had a tempo suited to a long-distance feat of endurance. Before the accordion joined the bagpipes as Scotland's national instrument, people danced to mouth music, unaccompanied songs where the rhythm mattered more than the words.

A different tempo was used by the women waulking cloth. A board would be set up on trestles and undyed cloth soaked in urine would be rhythmically pounded to shrink and fix the material. The process was the same as industrial fulling: fullers paid a small fee for the contents of chamber pots to supply the factories. Men were employed, you might say, to take the piss! Waulking cloth in the open air may not have been too bad but the stench in a fulling works must have been horrendous!

Flora and I danced together all evening and I sat with her family when the band slipped out to have a drink from a half-bottle to sustain their further exertions. It was the first time I had said more than *ciamer a tha thu?* when we met or *tapadh leat* to her little sister Moira. She had just started secondary school and she had a massive crush on her English teacher who was sitting across the room with his wife and two year old son. Moira looked as if she expected him to leave them and come over to her, drawn by the magnetism of her adoration!

Her father and I got on really well. I think he was glad to talk to a man, even a very young one, as an antidote to sharing a croft house with a wife and three daughters. I always tried to get to their croft in time to walk Flora to her waitressing shift in the tearoom and he had taken to waylaying me when I arrived. He would stand at the door of the byre at about the time I was expected, trying to look as if it was just by chance.

"She's not ready yet. Come in and have a seat for a minute – she'll know where to find you."

So we would sit on crates and put the World to rights until Flora breezed in, kissed her Father just below his receding hairline and grabbed me by the hand. He was a martyr to sciatica so he would half rise then settle back onto his crate with a grimace of pain. I looked up sciatica in a medical dictionary and it sounded really painful!

I was a bit serious – well, all right, I was more than a little pompous. Flora could be serious especially on subjects close to her heart like the plight of children in the third World. The difference was that the rest of the time she was lively and happy. She brought out a side in me I hardly knew existed although I am still not sure why she bothered. I am very glad, though, that she did!

On the Monday morning after the ceilidh, when he sat down her Dad grimaced with the pain and started massaging his right buttock. I sympathised and asked if there was anything I could do.

"Thank you, but no. It will ease in a minute and I have taken one of my pain killers. Living in a house of women I get scant sympathy! I dare say women do have a harder life with periods and all that sort of thing – I know that Morag used to be in agony every month – but even so it would be nice to get a kind word about my own affliction."

I told him I knew very little about pain. "Is it as bad as toothache?"

Worse, he told me, so I asked if he really thought women experienced more pain or if it was just that men were better at handling agony.

"I could tell you a story about that – but you are too young!"

Saying I was too young had my hackles up and I might have gone into a huff but at that moment a commotion started in the house. Clearly there were people shouting but at first we could not distinguish what was being said.

Next moment the door opened and Moira stormed out with her mother at her heels. As she turned to continue the argument I could not avoid noticing that Moira could hardly keep her eyes from closing because of the weight of mascara on her lashes; her school skirt had been rolled up at the waist so that even standing she was only just covering her knickers.

They had just started what was obviously a reprise of entrenched positions about appropriate school dress when there was a clattering on the stairs and Flora erupted onto the stage. It appeared that she had detected the source of the cosmetics disfiguring Moira's eyes and she started to complain in immoderate language at the top of her voice.

Their Mother, who had been ripping Moira's character to shreds, now turned on Flora and began to abuse her for being selfish and cruel. Moira began to look a bit happier now there was a new target for the maternal wrath, but her Mother took time off to order her indoors to scrub her face.

"If I have to do it I will leave you red raw!" were her last words to the departing girl. Flora used this opportunity to slip back into the house, their Mother followed and the door was shut. I suppose the whole, stunning, action lasted less than a minute.

"You and I will just sit here and saw wood," her Father said. He must have noticed my puzzled look for he went on to explain. Early in their marriage, long before the children were born, he was losing a domestic argument and the only way he could think to escape his wife's tongue lashing was to say he had work to do out on the croft. He told her he had to go and saw wood and ever since he had used the same excuse whenever domestic problems threatened to overwhelm him. It was so much an accepted family tradition that even Moira would tell him to saw wood if he was upset by her behaviour – as he not infrequently was!

After the dramatics we sat in silence watching the croft door but staying well back in the shadows. When the school bus arrived, Moira slammed out of the front door with her face pink and her school skirt a millimetre or two longer than the rules required.

A minute later, Flora exited closing the door after her with exaggerated care.

"Are you in there, Daddy?" she called as she came towards the byre. He had only time to whisper: "It's serious if she's calling me 'Daddy'."

Flora bounced in and threw her arms around his neck, gave a few choking sobs and asked if he thought it was fair that she was being abused because Moira had stolen her favourite mascara.

"You are always telling us to be honest and respect each other, Daddy."

"Not long ago you did exactly the same thing to Morag, I remember."

She jumped up, her face flaming and her eyes flashing.

"How can you be so unfeeling, Father?" she sobbed.

I had stood up when she came in, and I now moved forward to escort her to work.

"And you can just sit down again. You're just another man and I hate all men!"

She was out the door before my jaw had stopped dropping but as I moved to go after her I was pulled back.

"Just saw wood, lad."

I was shattered. It was our first quarrel and I had done nothing and said nothing to upset her!

"Did you enjoy the ceilidh?"

The last thing on my mind was the ceilidh. I could feel the tears prickling in my eyes when I thought of Flora and me dancing the whole night without a care. Was it all over between us? What about our plans for spending the rest of our lives together? With an effort, I pulled myself together.

"Oh, yes, the ceilidh. Well, it was OK – no, I mean it was great. I thought my Uncle's song about the monkey was funny although I didn't really understand all the funny bits."

Flora's Father sat with his hands between his knees staring into space. He showed no more interest in the answer than I had shown in the question.

"The four women in my home get on really well for almost all of the time. Then there comes a day, and today is one of them, when out of the blue they are at each other's throats.

"It is best to let them come out of it in their own way in their own time – without any interference from the men in their lives. If you had gone after her, Flora would likely have said some wounding things and she might not have been able to say sorry when she calmed down – she is a proud girl. Just you sit here for another ten minutes then go and see your Gran – I promise that she won't be the only one that's glad to see you.

"The ironical thing is that Flora will more than likely buy the same mascara for Moira out of her tips!"

So I sat, sawing wood, and then went to the tearoom where Flora dazzled me with a beaming smile and a rib-breaking hug. Being a scientist of sorts, I wanted to understand what had happened but Gran overheard and chased me out to fix the damned awning again. "It's women's stuff," she told me. "There is no man who ever lived who will ever understand us so just be thankful that Flora still loves you!"

Uncle James was no more help when I put the case before him on appeal from the lower court.

"It's just women. The trouble in Eden wasn't because of an apple or even the snake, it was putting Eve in there with nothing to do but make life difficult for poor Adam."

Chapter Twenty-One: *The Final Nail*

The folk on the island often seemed old fashioned to me when I started going there at first, coming, as I did, from the mighty city of Glasgow. There certainly are some differences between town and country but, as I got older, I recognised that they were largely superficial; more a difference of style than of substance.

There is much less crime on the island than in the city but a certain lawlessness is not only tolerated but applauded. Almost anything that discomfits the government or local authority is met with an approving nod. It is beyond their understanding that anyone should claim ownership of wild deer on the hills, salmon in the rivers and water fowl camping out on the machair during their migratory journey.

There are, of course, strict local rules about lawlessness as about every other aspect of life on the island. Take a stag or a cock salmon for yourself and your friends and you will be supported by the whole population: including an alibi if you should need it. Killing for commercial gain is a different matter. If you drop a fish off at the back door of the local hotel in return for a few drinks your actions will be accepted by the majority but you will have to take your chances with water bailiffs and police. Selling regularly for money is frowned upon and the locals will have a quiet word; ignore the warning and they might well shop you to the authorities.

Moderation is the key. Anything organised on a commercial scale will attract too much attention: do not rub the noses of the landowners into the muck and trust that they will let you continue with your modest larceny in peace. Moderation is the touchstone of much of island life. Extremes are mistrusted whether the outcome is excessively good or bad. The guiding principle is to do no hurt to your neighbours. A melee while the blood is quickened by strong drink is, of course, perfectly acceptable!

If someone wants to dress in animal pelts, often imperfectly cured, and live in a cave half way up a mountain, the locals will wish him the best of luck and keep a friendly eye out for his welfare. But if he tries to dress his children in skins and involve them in his Neanderthal lifestyle, the community will step in and put a stop to it.

Muggings and theft are rare because they cause distress to other people. Either they will be neighbours or the visitors that are so vital to the economy. The only exception allowed is the institutionalised mugging and theft perpetrated by tourist shops selling cheap tat at exorbitant prices! The islanders have great sympathy and some respect for white settlers who arrive with an urge to make candles or hand-weave cloth from wool they have themselves carded and spun.

"Nice enough to look at," as Uncle James says. "But you get better quality at half the price in the Coop."

As I stuttered through my teenage years, I began to realise that the main difference between the lifestyles of the city and island lay in anonymity. In the city you can live next door to someone for twenty years without knowing their name or what they do for a living. The person you mug or burgle is a complete stranger so you can easily convince yourself that your actions are justified.

On the island nothing is secret or private. When you arrive, the locals want to know all about you, your family and your antecedents back to, at least, Noah. What you do not tell them they will make up, so it is usually safer to tell the truth.

The consequences are stark. In the city it is possible for someone to lie dead in a tenement flat for weeks before anyone notices that the air in the close is becoming rank. On the island people are cared for. There was one old lady who lived alone by the grace of her neighbours. On his way to meet the first boat, the bus driver took in a bottle of milk and made tea that he took to old Jeanette in bed. The postman looked in whether or not there was mail to deliver to her, then the lady that ran the newsagent shop locked the door after the morning rush was over and called on Jeanette to get her washed, dressed and settled in her chair at the window where she could see what was going on in the town. The newsagent came back later to get Jeanette ready for bed. During the day the old lady was brought meals and snacks by friends who would stay for half an hour to chat.

When I was in my last year at school I worked in the early evening delivering pizzas, often to a population of single mothers living in a large ghetto in the city. The orders phoned in to the shop were placed in a small van and driven to a central distribution point in the high rise wasteland. Two of us ran up and down stairs delivering the boxed delicacies; the van driver rode shotgun on his vehicle to ensure that it kept its full complement of wheels and wing mirrors.

I quickly learned that an open blouse and deep cleavage signalled a determined attempt to pay for the pizzas with something other than coin of the realm. I was only fourteen when I started so they may just have been trying to mother me!

"Oh there ye are. My aren't you the wee charmer then. A bet you've broke a few hearts."

When her arm stretched out to take a firm grip of the pizza box, a bra strap always seemed to slip causing the abundant flesh generously displayed, to quiver.

"Just come in for a wee minute till a find ma purse."

I had been warned to keep a tight hold on the box and to brace myself at this stage to avoid losing the pizza or being hauled in bodily, pizza and all! There was always a draft of hot air coming through the open door carrying a smell of cheap scent overlying something much earthier. It reminded me of Johnson's baby powder battling with the stench of a shitty nappy when my wee sister was a baby.

I had been prepared for my first night on the job by Willie, a worldly cynic of fifteen, who took me round with him for a couple of nights before I flew solo up and down the stairs. Every block had at least two lifts but the only people who expected them to work were Martians newly landed and Council officers responsible for maintaining the buildings. Both groups were disappointed but only the Council was surprised.

Willie was only propositioned about one call in three but I seemed to get offers at every single flat! I don't know whether I was just unlucky but I expect my naivety was all too evident.

Even if there had been time, the offers were less than appealing. At fifty pence for a delivery, you had to run and keep running to make your shift worthwhile. There was the added incentive that if you dawdled the van driver would leave you behind to face a two mile walk through Indian Territory back to the shop, and the local Apaches were always on the warpath!

At fourteen my hormones were kicking in but I was still fastidious. Because of my age, I was on the early shift so I saw the ladies in dishabille, which translates as curlers, joggers, scuffed slippers and, more often than not, stained bras. When I turned sixteen and was able to work later in the evening, I often saw them glammed up for a night out. I was sorely tempted on occasions but the thought of the long walk back to the shop kept me pure. To resist temptation, I had a mantra that I repeated over and over in my head: 'curlers, slippers, dirty bra.'

There are single mums amongst the islanders too, but they seem to be more realistic, perhaps because they can see the whole playing field. In the city, all the ladies expect prince charming to be the next man in their lives. In practice there is a sub-species of men who move about from single mum to single mum. Typically he starts off as the man of her dreams and her partner for life. Then, just about the time when the social catch up with the cohabitation and stop all her benefits, he moves to another mum in another close. The deserted woman has then to fight Social Services to get her allowances reinstated. It is not only boxers who 'float like a butterfly, sting like a bee'.

On the island, the girls can see all too clearly that the next candidate to fill her fireside chair is just the same kind of useless apology for a man that she tried and discarded last time. I suspect that there is a buoyant market in widowers with a steady job, at least up to late middle age.

In the older generation, separations and divorce do happen but the islanders seem to try a bit harder before they accept the inevitable and part. One of James' neighbours, married for almost thirty-five years, had drifted into alcoholic inertia. He spent most of his time sitting in an armchair beside the peat fire burning brightly summer and winter. He would go out from time to time to join his cronies for a wee libation in the hotel returning on the verge of collapse with enough bottles to save him having to brave the elements for a day or two.

"At one time he was a connoisseur of whisky," James told me. "He could not only identify single malts but he could tell which of them had been used to mix with grain spirits to make blended whisky. He always said that you could only do it once or twice before your palette became jaded."

Now he was reduced to buying the cheapest form of booze available.

His wife had become accustomed to the life.

"He was a fine, handsome man when we got married," she confided to Aunt Effie. "He was a good provider and he gave me two wonderful children. It's just that in the last few years I have had to pay a very high price."

It was after the children were grown up and had left home that the deterioration had started. For some years, his drinking was intermittent with periods of sobriety between the binges, but the intervals had become shorter and shorter. During his sober spells he was remorseful and did jobs about the house and croft to appease his wife and conscience. Between them they had agreed a plan, starting with the kitchen and bathroom and due to reach its climax with the retiling of the roof.

Progress became stuttering, finally juddering to a halt with the roof tiles stacked beside the byre covered with a tarpaulin. For some time she used the periods when the alcoholic haze was less dense to prod him into action but he simply produced a string of excuses to avoid starting the roofing project. She bought a slater's hammer, special nails and padded guards that he could strap on to protect his knees. All to no avail.

At that stage he was forced to play his ace: there was no ladder on the croft long enough to reach the eaves. It took his long suffering wife some time and much thought before she found a card to play, but it was the Ace of trumps!

"I'm going to the night school this winter," she told Effie.

"I was thinking of going myself. There's an embroidery class and they're saying that if there's enough support they'll put on a lace-making class – tatting, I think they call it. If we were going to the same class we could share the driving and it would be company on the road."

"That would have been lovely, Effie, but I'm going to the woodworking class. I'm going to make a roof ladder so that my no good husband will have no excuse for leaving the roof leaking!"

"Did she do it?" I asked Uncle James.

"She certainly did. In fact it's that ladder hanging on the wall of the byre. She turned all the rungs on a lathe and made the joints as tight as a master craftsman. A beautiful ladder altogether."

"How does it come to be in your byre?"

"Well her husband still wouldn't tackle the job. Maybe he thought he would fall off since his balance wasn't what it had been. In any event it was me and Neil Post that did the roof and she gave me the ladder for a present."

"So that must have been the last nail in the coffin of their marriage," I mused, straying into poetic language in the heat of the moment.

"No at all. The last nail turned out to be a toenail. She found it and several more with fluff balls and bogeys in the drawer of his bedside table when she was spring cleaning. She packed a bag and left the same day."

Chapter Twenty-Two: *Ven Villages*

Uncle James got a phone call from the laird about a month after I had taken him to Chester railway station to catch a train to London. He was going there to get legal advice from an old colleague about a decision by the local council to increase the size of the island's tiny airstrip to accommodate passenger jets. The colleague is a lady and was, according to the laird, on the point of being made a judge.

"I think he has a bit of a fancy for the lady judge," I suggested to James.

His reply: "The laird has more sense," was drowned by a chorus from Gran and Aunt Effie. "I hope he has enough sense to propose to her – he could just be doing with a good woman in his life."

Uncle James attempted a stout defence of the laird's common sense but the ladies ignored him while they worked out the logistics of bringing the man to the starting line. They concluded that it would have to be done by them unless the judge took matters into her own hands.

"He's too much of a gentleman," Gran concluded.

"Aye, he could do with a wee touch of his own father's roving eye. My, but the old gentleman had a way with the ladies!" Effie added, preening herself and getting a rather far-away look in her eye.

James stomped out at that point and I trailed after him so I missed all the salacious details about the old laird that Gran demanded from her sister-in-law. They would have clammed up if I had stayed, so I missed nothing by leaving.

"At least in a trial they read out the charges before they condemn you," James opined. "The laird's only misdemeanour is that he is single – a condition that seems to drive women-folk wild."

The prolonged absence in London fuelled speculation on the island and you could get no better odds than two to one on that the laird would come back engaged to be married. Even the firm assertion by Uncle James that the man knew better than to become embroiled would not induce him to risk a bet.

The phone rang as James was passing so he picked it up. He and the laird exchanged pleasantries for a minute or two then talked about the weather and the cattle for a few minutes more before James listened in complete silence, nodding occasionally, while the laird was obviously giving detailed instructions.

"I'll send the lad," James said at last and then he replaced the receiver.

He had only just reached the phone before Effie who could show a fair turn of foot when she wanted to. Throughout she stood close beside her husband trying to hear what the laird was saying. James, being a wee bit deaf, held the receiver crushed against his ear so no sound leaked out. Effie hopped from foot to foot and kept pulling his sleeve and mouthing questions she wanted answers to.

"Well, what did he say?" she demanded before the receiver had settled in its rest.

"He just phoned to ask if we could pick him up at the airstrip tomorrow when the plane from Glasgow gets in."

"Why didn't you ask him what he had been up to all this time? You're as useless as the rest of the men. Did he say nothing else?"

James looked puzzled and pushed up his cap to scratch his head.

"Well now, he was asking after you – 'is Effie all right?' he said. Oh and he asked if we would take the big car instead of the Land Rover."

Effie had her coat on and was out the door in her slippers while James stood and gaped at her. He came round to my wee house in the old byre a few minutes later to ask me if I would take the Volvo to the airstrip the next day. He was still puzzling over Effie's behaviour.

"It's obvious," I said. "If the laird was coming on his own the Land Rover would have been good enough. Since he specified the big car he must have company – probably of the female persuasion if he thinks luxury is needed."

"By Jove, boy, I think you've got it. If you go on like this I might have to reconsider my opinion of you as a book-learned geek with no common sense!"

Next day I was at the airport in plenty of time to have a crack with Angus before he climbed the outside stair to become the island's air traffic controller. Later he would be the baggage handler after he had used the Day-Glo paddles that were his pride and joy to usher the arriving aircraft into the sole parking slot.

I went back to the car when he climbed to the control tower just as the minister's old car pulled up beside the Volvo. Mr and Mrs Dinwoody were in the back: he had been getting a bit frail so the Assembly sent an apprentice minister to help him out. He would be a nice lad when he had finally come to terms with having ginger hair: he told me that he had tried keeping it very short but it looked even more bizarre with pink scalp showing through the ginger.

He was driving and he hopped out as soon as the car stopped to help the old couple to alight. Mrs Dinwoody thanked him graciously with her customary twinkle, stopping just short of outright laughter but the minister grumped that he could manage on his own and then nearly fell flat when he tripped over his walking stick.

By the time this little drama had ended, Angus had the plane neatly parked, had opened the door and was unfolding the integral steps. First out was the laird backing down with his hand held out into the aircraft cabin. The hand that reached out of the dimness to grasp it was small with a glitter of rings. In to our view, stepped a mature lady beautifully dressed in a tailored suit. She was smiling sweetly and, it seemed to me, she held on to the laird's hand for several heartbeats longer than was strictly necessary.

Next moment the crowning drama of the day erupted from the aircraft. We first saw a veil of shiny auburn hair bent forward to get through the door. As she emerged she straightened to her full height. She must have been five foot ten in her stockings but she had chosen to wear five inch heels so she towered over all of us when she stepped down.

I was aware of a little disturbance beside me but before I could turn to see if the minister was still on his feet, the amazon turned and ran at me full tilt with a maniacal grin on her face!

After a pace or two she stopped to take off her heels so she could reach me faster. She pelted on with her skirt flapping above her shapely knees and a stiletto in each hand pointed straight at my face.

I am not a fast thinker in such emergencies and I was still trying to decide whether to try to defend myself or turn tail and head for the hills when she ran past me without even noticing I was there: her target was the Dinwoody's!

"Mum! Dad!" she shrieked like a maenad as she hurtled past to envelop the old couple in a bear hug.

The laird approached at a more sedate pace ushering his lady with a hand possessively on the small of her back. By the time they reached us the minister was standing alone with a big grin on his face while his wife and daughter, still welded together, did a sort of jitterbug.

"This is Helen," the laird began warmly shaking the minister's hand. And this, my dear, is the Reverend Doctor Dinwoody and his wife. His daughter you already know."

Letting go her Mum, Heather Dinwoody put her arm round her Dad and turned to Helen. "Don't forget he's a minister. If you call him a vicar he'll likely excommunicate you!"

Eventually everyone but the apprentice got into the big car and I drove them first to the manse where we had morning coffee, then we all piled in again and I took them to the big house for lunch. Ginger had collected all of the luggage and delivered it so when he arrived to eat and, eventually, run the Dinwoody's home, I was able to get away.

"It is very simple, really - but a bit complicated," was my brilliant opening statement to an audience of Gran, Effie, all the waitresses and half the women on the island with Uncle James trying to look as if he was not as interested as the rest. I had gone, of course, directly from the laird's house to the tearoom to make my report.

"The laird and Helen worked together years ago. She had a husband at that time but they were fond of each other - fond enough, the laird said, to keep him single while he waited for her." I was almost drowned out by female sighs when I told them this bit. "She is now a widow," brought more sighs.

"Anyway. She was happy to help but knowing next to nothing about Scots law in general and nothing at all about the Crofters Acts she started thinking about who she knew that could help. Then she remembered a young Writer she had worked with a year or two before. This girl was an expert in Scots law and an authority on Crofting legislation. It was only when they met her in Edinburgh that the laird realised it was the minister's girl."

"I suppose I had been told her married name but if so I had totally forgotten it," he explained to us.

I had barely finished when gran summed up the mood of the meeting: "Well then, is the laird engaged or not?"

So I told them of the hand holding and the 'my dear'. They thought things were promising but not yet conclusive.

"The laird is such a gentleman that he would treat her like that even if he couldn't stand the sight of her."

"You couldn't use that story if you were writing a book," I said to Uncle James sometime later when we had escaped the throng. "Your readers would just laugh at all the coincidences."

"More fool them; coincidences happen all the time in real life. I mind in school we had things called ven diagrams. For example you put the names of all the weans with a bike in a circle and the ones with roller skates in another. In the middle there was a wee egg-shaped bit where the circles overlapped that had the name of the spoiled brats with both."

"Ven diagrams are my bread and butter, Uncle James."

"That is as may be but have you ever thought of using ven diagrams on communities?"

His idea was that the people of the island formed a ven circle and that individual islanders were part of other ven communities, say stamp collectors or pigeon fanciers. I could see what he was getting at: I am part of the island group but I live in Glasgow and have friends from childhood, and more recently fellow students.

"It's a wee bit far-fetched, Uncle James."

"Not at all, not at all. Scotland is a wee country and the lives of most of us intersect. If you meet another Scot you will quickly find a person or a place in common."

He had first noticed this when he went to university, never before having left the island. He soon found that his classmates were not altogether the strangers they had appeared at first. They knew people he had met or they had visited the island: one boy even had an aunt living in the island capital.

He further developed the idea when he was aide to an admiral visiting naval establishments and spending time alone in strange messes. He would approach any Scot he met and challenge him to find a connection.

"It only failed once," he told me.

On a tour of recruiting offices they had stopped in a small town where the admiral was dining with a retired shipmate. James was left to amuse himself in the bar of the local hotel. A party of young men came in and when James heard that one of them spoke with a brogue he introduced himself. They had a drink together before James proposed his challenge to his fellow countryman.

"He put his drink down, less than half finished, turned on his heel and left the pub without a word to any of us. His friends called after him asking what was wrong and one of them even followed him out the door but he had vanished into the night.

"I have always wondered what dread secret the poor fellow had to hide."

Chapter Twenty-Three: *Dating Agencies*

"Do you know?" Uncle James asked me as we sat on the decking behind Gran's tearoom drinking tea. I was licking the tip of my finger so I could pick up the crumbs of cakes and scones that had lately filled the china plate on the table between us. The cream was no longer special since the wee problem Aunt Effie used to have had dried up.

"The programmes on the television are worse rubbish now than ever they was but the adver-ties-ments are really educational."

He was fidgeting around as he spoke, drumming his fingers one minute, smoothing the tablecloth the next and all the time shifting about in his chair. He was half way through the second day of his no-smoking regime and the strain was telling on him.

Before I could reply to his comment, he had jumped up, rattling the cups as he bumped into the table in his haste. He was heading through the bead curtain into the tearoom proper before my jaw had finished dropping.

"Well then, are you coming? I'm going for a walk and a young fellow like you needs more exercise!" he was still mumbling about students sitting about all day or holding hands with girls, when I followed him out. I was nearly as jittery as he was since Flora had gone to Glasgow shopping with her mother and they were planning to spend two or three nights in Morag's flat in Kelvindale.

"Will it be two nights then or will it be three?" I asked in my most petulant voice.

"Oh for heaven's sake! We're not joined at the hip. If you're like this now what will it be like when we're married?" Flora flounced into the car – not an easy thing to do – leaving me slowly analysing what she had said; at least she still wanted to marry me even if she did not have a very high opinion of me!

Uncle James and I had been getting on each other's nerves all afternoon. Our usual easy friendship and instinctive understanding seemed to have been just a romantic pipedream. Now that I had no romance and he had given up his pipe we were scratching around each other like two old roosters.

It took me nearly ten minutes to catch James, who had marched off along the sheep track above the beach; it is only fair to admit that I was in no great rush to close the gap. I started to slow down when he did but then gave myself a shake: we were behaving in such a ridiculous way that I began laughing and broke into a run to pull up alongside my Uncle. Typically, he continued talking about television disregarding the quarter hour that had elapsed since he introduced the topic.

"Everyone seems to want to save me money. In the old days the Hydro Board put up pylons, strung wires and put in a meter. If you wanted light you used their electricity or a hurricane lamp; you could build up the fire to make your tea or just flick a wee switch. Simple – not cheap but clean and convenient.

"There are no more pylons that I can see but now there are a dozen companies competing to supply my needs. How do they know at the power station that it is going to be me that fancies a *strupach* when the current gets to the island?

"Do you think they send out the electric in wee parcels with my name on the label? I just hope they don't leave it to Neil Post to deliver them!"

The latest scandal on the island was that Neil had delivered a plain brown envelope addressed to H. McTavish, the pier master, to A McTavish, a holier-than-thou lay preacher. Mind you, it took nearly a week for the preacher to return the magazine containing, so I was told, graphic descriptions of unorthodox sexual practices!

"It's all just make believe by the government. They really want everything bigger, more centralised, but they kid us that we have individual choice. It won't be politicians that eventually unite the human race; it will be the result of a merger between the Bank of America and the National Bank of China.

"If they really wanted things to be small and local they could start by making us use alternative energy. The tide rises and falls three or four feet twice a day around the island and the wind blows your cap off six days out of seven: we could make a fortune exporting electricity without oxygenating a single carbon atom!"

We walked on in companionable silence for several minutes before James returned to his theme of television adverts.

"Then there's these 'dating agencies', as they call themselves. Old women of eighty advertising for youngsters in their sixties – toy boys, they call them. You have to put in a recent picture or they won't even look at your application."

Now my attention was roused; they certainly show moony couples to advertise dating agencies on television but Uncle James must have delved into the subject a lot further. He is always saying that computers are beyond his understanding but I am beginning to wonder if he is a closet Silver Surfer.

As he stopped speaking he reached into his pocket. Usually at the start of one of his streams of consciousness it he would pause while his audience came to attention to fill his pipe with tobacco and get it drawing to his satisfaction. This evening there was no pipe, no tobacco and a look of despair crossed his face that wrung my heart.

"I think the agencies would be for people who have moved to a new part of the country and don't know anyone," I suggested, giving him time to pull himself together.

"I sometimes wish that I lived in a place where nobody knew me.

The trouble with the island is that we all know each other far too well! If one more old biddy gives me a sympathetic smile, pats me on the shoulder and says 'you're a brave lad, James, givin' up the pipe after all these years' I might be forced to consider enlisting in the French Foreign Legion."

"Have you been at the Beau Geste?"

"Och well, there was nothing much on the telly so I just watched the film this morning."

We had wandered down onto the shore and were strolling along the tideline turning over interesting bits of flotsam with the toes of our boots. Finding nothing that was worth a closer look, we went further out since the tide was at the full ebb.

"See these timbers just showing through the sand?" James pointed to two pillars each about a metre high covered in barnacles and festooned with seaweed and bunches of mussels.

"Are they timbers? I often wondered but never thought to ask."

"They are all that is left of a ship of the line that fought for Britain at the time of Nelson. After the Napoleonic wars she was fitted with a coal-fired boiler and propeller before taking part in the blockade of the Russian Baltic ports during the Crimean disagreement.

"After that she was sold to a Glasgow firm that did her up to carry immigrants to America but they went bust so she ended up here. You might say that she became the Victorian version of a Dating Agency!"

James was grinning at me, but he still looked a bit forlorn and was having trouble deciding what to do with his hands: at this stage in the story he should be reaming out his pipe and reloading it, giving me time to speculate on the connection between an old wooden ship and matrimony.

"Up until about 1960, herring were abundant in the seas around Britain. A creature of very regular habits, the herring; they swim clockwise around the coast arriving at the same time every year – until their numbers started to dwindle and they stopped coming all together. Trawlers from all over Europe and beyond pulled them out the sea by the thousands. Far too many were caught to be eaten fresh so most of them were salted or kippered.

"That's where the old hulk came into its own!"

Girls from fishing communities lived in the cabins designed for immigrants. They spent the days gutting herring and laying them down in barrels of coarse salt. When the herring moved on, one of the trawlers would take the hulk in tow, with many of the girls still on board, to the next harbour around the coast.

"It was good money for the girls. They could earn nothing at home except maybe a pittance from carding wool but the reason most of them stayed on board was for the adventure and the matrimonial prospects."

When the trawlers were working the girls were gutting from dawn to dusk but there were times when the catch was poor or the trawlers were moving to a new location when they were able to clean themselves up, put on whatever finery they could find and go ashore to dance.

"I think the notion that alcohol lowers the inhibitions of young women is a myth they put about just to get free drinks. If you really want a lass to be putty in your hands, dance with her. Not quick-steps and waltzes, mind you, although I daresay they were well enough for the effete women of Vienna. If you want to arouse the passion in a Highland girl get her on the floor for Strip the Willow or The Dashing White Sergeant!

"Wherever they went ashore they were mobbed. Fine sturdy young girls that knew the meaning of work: they were snapped up by fisher lads from Oban to Great Yarmouth. They would find themselves in front of a vicar saying 'I do' before the herring blood had dried on their gutting knives!

"There was never any danger of in-breeding when the shoals of silver herring were about!"

Chapter Twenty-Four: *Step We Gaily*

Despite all the intrigue and manoeuvring by Gran and Aunt Effie, it was Mrs Dinwoody who found out the laird's intentions. She used a strategy never even contemplated by the islanders: she asked him straight out!

On the day he brought Helen to the island with the Dinwoody's daughter they were in the drawing room of the big house waiting for lunch to be served.

The two legal ladies were discussing tort and the shocking lack of dusting that was evident in this main public room. They were at odds on the relative merits of the Scottish and English legal systems but they were united in their opinion that the laird was far too soft with his staff.

The minister had been fretting so I had gone with him to the front door to wait for the ginger-headed assistant minister.

"I hope he's all right. That car of mine can be quite temperamental, you know. He is just a boy really and with such beautiful hair."

He said this totally sincerely and without a trace of irony. Mr Dinwoody would find something good to say about Satan!

The laird had gone to the drawing room window where he was tutting over the neglected state of the garden when the minister's wife joined him.

"Now then, Henry. Are you and Helen planning to tie the knot?"

The laird blushed to his bald spot and while he struggled to articulate a response, Helen came across to join them. Mrs Dinwoody had so many deaf parishioners that her normal speaking voice often caused a stir under the turf in the graveyard.

"Come on then, Henry, answer the lady. They have abolished hanging and I can't even sentence you to transportation to the colonies. So, what do you say?"

The laird dropped to his knees, clutched Helen's hand and began to stammer out a proposal. Before he got beyond describing the honour her Honour would do him, Helen dropped to her knees in front of him and kissed him squarely on the lips.

"It was a most satisfactory sort of kiss," Mrs Dinwoody reported later. "Fond – you could even say adoring – but with a strong undertone of passion suppressed with almost superhuman restraint."

"Sounds more like Mills and Boon than the laird," as Uncle James observed when he heard about it.

The embrace ended when the laird's knees gave an audible crack.

"Get your husband in here quick to ratify the decision of the court before our knees are permanently knackered."

In the event, they decided that the wedding should take place in London in an Anglican church. The first plan was going to involve flying two plane loads of islanders down for the ceremony but a happy chance allowed for a more elegant solution.

Flora's sister, Morag, my first crush on the island, had a flat in Glasgow she shared with an amiable micro-biologist. It was a closely guarded secret so, of course, everyone on the island knew they were living together: you might, therefore, find it hard to imagine the furore that Morag's youngest sister caused when she casually mentioned the cohabitation at a church social!

A week after the laird almost proposed and was comprehensively accepted, Morag phoned home to announce that she and Graham were planning to marry on the island in three months' time.

"Who's Graham?" Morag's father was reported to have said when he heard the news.

"I was only kidding," he confided to me later. "It's the usual problem in this house: too many women and not one with a sense of humour."

It was the minister who first suggested that the couples hold a joint ceilidh after the nuptials. The idea was approved without a dissenting voice although it took more than a month to find a compromise plan and to smooth all the feathers ruffled in the process. Those who felt most deeply that their ideas had been ignored remained somewhat tender in their feelings right up to the big day.

James and Effie were the only ones from the island to attend the London wedding: James was the best man. Helen's son by her first marriage gave her away and her daughter was matron of honour. Half the members of the judiciary were guests.

"They looked very ordinary without their gowns and wigs," Effie recorded in a disappointed tone. "You wouldn't give them the same respect if they just wore their suits in the court."

Back on the island I was an usher on the bride's side, keeping a very beady eye on the best man just in case he had designs on Flora, the chief bridesmaid.

"He's more likely to fancy you than me," Flora reassured me in her most exasperated tone. "He's gay."

I was not totally convinced because, in my opinion, Flora would cause a stir in the loins of a marble statue. How gay was he, I wondered – there must surely be degrees of gayness?

Gran told me to 'away and bile yer can'.

"Flora is as mad about you as you are about her – if it wasn't for that blind spot she would be perfect!"

Helen and the laird brought a plane load of guests up from London, including her two grown-up children. Uncle James was allowed to use the public address in the plane to prepare them for their visit to Ultima Thule and so I think they were disappointed when they landed to find that we all stood more or less erect and only a small proportion grazed their knuckles when they walked.

Everything went well after we adjusted to the speed of their speech.

"One fellow gave me such a tongue lashing," Flora's dad told me. "At least it sounded like a telling off although I did not understand one word in four. Blow me, but when he finished his litany of complaint he gave me a big grin, shook my hand and clapped me on the shoulder!"

We sent the visitors round the island in a bus so we could finalise the preparations for the evening. The laird insisted on acting as the courier.

"I don't want James filling their heads with any more nonsense. They're English and so have no more than a vestigial sense of humour and no knowledge of anything that happens beyond the last station on the London Underground."

Flora was fully occupied at the church and the reception. She looked stunningly beautiful, of course, and she performed her duties to perfection. The best man proved that he was sufficiently gay to exonerate him of evil intentions. Although largely a spectator, I quite enjoyed the day, day-dreaming about a time when I would take a lead role alongside Flora.

Excitement mounted as the time for the ceilidh approached. The four principals and their chief attendants had dinner in the restaurant of the councillor/hotelier who had started all the trouble by proposing the runway extension. The laird made a rambling speech, according to Uncle James, that effectively thanked the man who had brought Helen into our lives for being a wee nyaff.

The hotelier missed the implications, for the next day when I met him he was crowing about being the laird's new best friend! Even after all his years on the island he is just a White Settler when all is said and done.

The ceilidh was like no other the island had experienced. Clifford, who was a fair tenor in the rather florid Welsh style, joined forces with a soprano friend of Morag's who was in the chorus at Scottish Opera; she sang several solo arias and admirably supported Clifford in some duets. They were accompanied by the best man who had just failed to make it as a concert pianist.

The sous chef fiddler from the band turned out to be an

accomplished violinist. He was joined on stage by the council official who had tried to close down the tearoom. He had fixed up all the documentation and had become a great favourite with Gran. He brought his cello and the pair entertained us with selections from Vivaldi and Mozart.

The locals sang a few of the better known Gaelic songs and, when the consumption of alcohol passed the critical point, the Londoners accepted instruction and were able to join the islanders in a rendition of 'Marie's Wedding' the like of which had never been heard before (we can only pray that it is not repeated).

Heather, the minister's daughter, turned up in a micro dress with six inch heels, accompanied by her husband who is an international basketball player; he was the only man in the room who could look her in the eye! She had forced the council to withdraw their plans for developing the airstrip.

"The government cuts have left them so hard up that they were falling over themselves to withdraw the plans," she modestly admitted.

The dancing was a huge success until Flora's wee sister exercised her fascination with older men. She was smitten by a barrister with silver at his temples and finally plucked up the courage to ask him to dance.

"Delighted, my dear. You know, I have a daughter about your age."

Marie, predictably, stomped off in the huff followed by the teenage son of Neil Post who was sweet on her. Whatever he said worked for I discovered them snogging when I went round the back of the hall to join the lads for a wee refreshment.

Gran landed in the lap of a High Court judge when her demonstration of a pas-de-bas fell victim to age and alcohol. The judge's wife said Gran could have him if she could borrow James; Effie offered to go home and pack his bag so long as she would bring him back for the clipping.

"Is he the island hairdresser?" asked the judicial consort in accents slightly less cut-glass than at the outset – the cognoscenti were now able to detect a hint of Bermondsey creeping in.

At this point the conversation became, as they say, general.

"He once gave me a haircut – it wasn't too bad."

"I see you've had a touch of the sun – your bald spot's peeling."

"Nothing wrong with being a hairdresser!" This remark by the judge's wife was explained without discretion by her best friend: "He met her when she cut his hair in a salon off the Edgeware road when he was a struggling junior."

"Are you implying that you can look down on my bald spot? How dare you suggest that I am wee!"

Gran meanwhile was showing a disgraceful lack of urgency in getting off the judge's lap – in fact it looked like she was settling in for the rest of the evening.

Where it might have ended I cannot guess but the extra pressure of Gran sitting over his bladder forced the judge to rise and make for the toilet at something better than his usual stately speed.

About half past eleven Flora's Mum and Dad met us as we stepped off the floor after a particularly energetic eightsome reel.

One set was made up of Londoners and the other of locals so it quickly became very competitive. Helen's son, a promising young man newly called to the bar, exceeded escape velocity in the hands of an Essex girl but the visitors just carried on one short.

Uncle James picked him up and started to explain his theory of ven connections. His normal rather obscure delivery was further clouded by alcohol so the lad finished up thinking he had concussion.

The locals claimed a win by default since the Londoners were a man short but they insisted they had won a moral victory having finished more than half a bar ahead of the band.

"We're away to our beds, dear. It's been a long day – a happy day, of course, but long and tiring. Don't you be too late; I'll leave the door on the latch for you."

Flora clutched my arm so tight her fingers dug in and faced her

Mum. "I won't *be* home. I'm going to spend the night in the old byre. And while I'm about it I'll tell you now that we're going to be living together when we go back to the uni."

I was as gob-smacked as her Mum and Dad. It would help if she discussed things with me, I thought as I stood there like Chicken Little waiting for the sky to fall. There was an agonisingly long pause before her Dad grinned and kissed Flora on the cheek.

"It's the way things are now, Mother. Our blessings on the pair of you."

He put his arm about his wife's shoulder and steered her towards the door talking earnestly all the time. I do not know what he said but just before they exited Flora's Mum turned and gave us a rather tentative smile and a wee wave.

"Are you dancin'?"

"Are you askin'?"

"I'm askin'."

"Then I'm dancin'."

Flora and I returned to the dance floor to celebrate our new life in partnership, openly acknowledged and approved.

And so *Oidhche math mo ghaol.*

About the Author

Originally from the Dalmuir area of Clydebank in Scotland, Alasdair McPherson is now retired and living in exile in Lincolnshire, England.

He says he has always wanted to write, but life got in the way until recently. He has already penned three historical novels – *Thoth: Divine Words*, *The Exodus: Aaron's Story* and *Pleasant Pastures* – and has been trying his hand at short stories.

His short stories can be read for free on McStorytellers, the Scots-connected short story website (http://www.mcstorytellers.com).